KT-151-841

ALL THE WRONG QUESTIONS

———

"Who Could That Be at This Hour?"
"When Did You See Her Last?"
"Shouldn't You Be in School?"
"Why Is This Night Different from All Other Nights?"

ADDITIONAL REPORTS

———

File Under: Thirteen Suspicious Incidents

ALL THE WRONG
QUESTIONS
?
4

"Why Is This Night Different from All Other Nights?"

LEMONY SNICKET

ART BY SETH

EGMONT

EGMONT

We bring stories to life

Why Is This Night Different from All Other Nights?
First published in Great Britain 2015
by Egmont UK Limited
The Yellow Building
1 Nicholas Road
London W11 4AN

Text copyright © 2015 Lemony Snicket
Art copyright © 2015 Seth

ALL THE WRONG QUESTIONS: Why Is This Night Different from All Other Nights?
by Lemony Snicket reprinted by arrangement with Charlotte Sheedy Literary Agency.

Illustrations published by arrangement with Little, Brown, and Company,
New York, New York, USA. All rights reserved.

The moral rights of the author and artist have been asserted

978 1 4052 5624 7

A CIP catalogue record for this book is available from the British Library.

Printed and bound in Italy.

47914/1

TO: B., P. Bellerophon
FROM: LS
FILE UNDER: Stain'd-by-the-Sea, accounts of; murder,
investigations of; Hangfire; Bombinating Beast
4/4
cc: VFDhq

CHAPTER ONE

There was a town, and there was a train, and there was a murder. I was on the train, and I thought if I solved the murder I could save the town. I was almost thirteen and I was wrong. I was wrong about all of it. I should have asked the question "Is it more beastly to be a murderer or to let one go free?" Instead, I asked the wrong question—four wrong questions, more or less. This is the account of the last.

I was in a small room, not sleeping and not

liking it. The room was called the Far East Suite, and it sat uncomfortably in the Lost Arms, the only hotel in town. It had a chest of drawers and a little table with a metal plate that was responsible for heating up a number of very bad meals. A puzzling shape on the ceiling was someone's idea of a light fixture, and a girl on the wall, holding an injured dog, was someone else's idea of a painting. There was one window and one shutter covering it, so the room was far too dark except in the morning. In the morning it was far too light.

But most of the room was a pair of beds, and most of what I didn't like slept in the larger one. Her name was S. Theodora Markson. I was her apprentice and she was my chaperone and the person who had brought me to the town of Stain'd-by-the-Sea in the first place. She had wild hair and a green automobile, and those are the nicest things I could think of to say about her. We'd had a fight over our last big case, which you can read about if you're the sort of person who likes to know about other people's fights. She was still mad at me and had informed me I was not allowed to be mad at her. We had not talked much lately, except when I occasionally asked her what the *S* stood for in her name and she occasionally replied, "Stop asking." That night she had announced to me that we were both going to bed early. There is nothing wrong with an early bedtime, as long as you do not insist that everyone has to go with you. Now her wild hair lay sprawled on the pillow like a mop had jumped off a roof, and she was snoring a snore I'd never heard before. It is lonely to lie on your bed, wide awake, listening to someone snore.

I told myself I had no reason to feel lonely. It was true I had a number of companions in Stain'd-by-the-Sea, people more or less my own age, who had similar interests. Our most significant interest was in defeating a villain named Hangfire. My associates and I had formed an ad hoc branch of the organization that had sent me to this town. "Ad hoc" means we were all alone and making it up as we went along. Hangfire worked in the shadows, scheming to get his hands on a statue of a mythical creature called the Bombinating Beast, so my friends and I had also started to keep our activities quiet, so that Hangfire would not find out about us. We no longer saw each other as much as we used to, but worked in solitude, in the hopes of stopping Hangfire and saving Stain'd-by-the-Sea.

The distant whistle of a train reminded me that so far my associates and I hadn't had much success. Stain'd-by-the-Sea was a town that had faded almost to nothing. The sea had been drained away to save the ink business, but now the ink business was draining away, and everything in town was going down the drain with it. The newspaper was gone. The only proper school had burned down, and the town's schoolchildren were being held prisoner. Hangfire

4

and his associates in the Inhumane Society had them hidden in Wade Academy, an abandoned school on Offshore Island, for some reason that was surely nefarious, a word which here means "wicked, and involving stolen honeydew melons and certain equipment from an abandoned aquarium." The town's only librarian, Dashiell Qwerty, had been framed for arson, so now the town's only police officers would take the town's only librarian out of his cell and put him on the town's only train, so he could stand trial in the city.

You know who else is in the city standing trial, I told myself, but thinking about my sister didn't make it any easier to get to sleep. Kit had been caught on a caper when I was supposed to be there helping her. I felt very bad about this, and kept writing her letters in my head. The preamble was always "Dear Kit," but then I had trouble. Sometimes I promised her I would get her out, but that was a promise I couldn't necessarily keep. Sometimes I told her that soon she would be free, but I didn't know if that was true. So I told her I was thinking of her, but that felt very meager, so I kept crumpling up these imaginary letters and throwing them into a very handsome imaginary trash can.

And then there's the one, I thought, who has stolen more sleep from you than all the rest. Ellington Feint, like me, was somewhat new in town, having come to rescue her father from Hangfire's clutches. She'd told me that she would do "anything and everything" to rescue him, and "anything and everything" turned out to be a phrase which meant "a number of terrible crimes." Her crimes had caught up with her, and now she was locked in Stain'd-by-the-Sea's tiny jail. The train is coming for her too, I told myself. Soon she will be transported through the outskirts of town and down into the valley that was once the floor of the ocean. She will ride past the Clusterous Forest, a vast, lawless landscape of seaweed that has managed to survive without water, and you might never see her again.

So many people to think about, Snicket, and still you are all alone.

The whistle blew again, louder this time, or perhaps it just seemed louder because Theodora's odd snoring had stopped. It had stopped because it wasn't snoring. She'd been pretending to be asleep. I closed my eyes and held still so I could find out why.

"Snicket?" she whispered in the dark room. "Lemony Snicket?"

I didn't make a sound. When pretending to be asleep, you should never fake snoring in front of people who may have heard your actual snores. You should simply breathe and keep still. There are a great number of circumstances in which this strategy is helpful.

"Snicket?"

I kept still and kept breathing.

"Snicket, I know you're awake."

I didn't fall for that old trick. I listened to Theodora sigh, and then, with a great creaking, she got out of bed and pattered to the bathroom. There was a click and a small stripe of light fell across my face. I let it. Theodora rustled around in the bathroom and then the light went out and she walked across the Far East Suite with her feet sounding different than they had. She'd put on her boots, I realized. She was going out in the middle of the night, just when the train was coming to a stop.

I heard the doorknob rattle and quit. She was giving me one last look. Perhaps I should have opened my eyes, or simply said, suddenly in the dark, "Good luck." It would have been fun to startle her like that. But I just let her walk out and shut the door.

I decided to count to ten to make sure she was really gone. When I reached fourteen, she opened the door again to check on me. Then she walked out again and knocked the door shut again and I counted again and then one more time and then I stood up and turned the light on and moved quickly. I was at a disadvantage because I was in my pajamas, and it took me a few moments to hurry into clothing. I put on a long-sleeved shirt with a stiff collar that was clean enough, and my best shoes and a jacket that matched some good thick pants with a very strong belt. I mention the belt for a reason. I walked quickly to the door and opened it and looked down the hallway to make sure she wasn't waiting for me, but S. Theodora Markson had never been that clever.

I looked back at the room. The star-shaped fixture shone down on everything. The girl with the dog with the bandaged paw gave me her usual frown, as if she were bored and hoped I'd give her a magazine. Had I known I was leaving the Far East Suite behind forever, I might have taken a longer look. But instead I just glanced at it. The room looked like a room. I killed the lights.

In the lobby were two familiar figures, but neither of them was my chaperone. One was the statue that was always there in the middle of the room, depicting a woman with no clothes or arms, and the other was Prosper Lost, the hotel's proprietor, who stood by the desk giving me his usual smile. It was a smile that meant he would do anything to help you, anything at all, as long as it wasn't too much trouble.

"Good evening, Mr. Snicket."

"Good evening," I told him back. "How's your daughter, Lost?"

"If you hadn't decided to go to bed early, you would have seen her," Prosper told me. "She stopped by to visit me, and left something for you as well."

"Is that so?" I said. Ornette Lost was one of my associates, and for reasons I didn't quite understand, she lived with her uncles,

Stain'd-by-the-Sea's only remaining firefighters, instead of with her father.

"That is so," her father said now, and reached into his desk to retrieve a small object made of folded paper. I picked it up just as the whistle blew again.

It was a train.

"Ornette's always been good at fashioning extraordinary things out of ordinary materials," Lost said. "I suppose it runs in the family. Her mother had a great interest in sculpture."

"Did she?" I said, although I was not really listening. When someone leaves a folded paper train for you, you take a moment to wonder why.

"She did indeed," Lost said. "Alice had an enormous collection of statues and a great number of her own sculptures as well. They were displayed in the Far West Wing of this very hotel. My wife hoped the glyptotheca would attract tourists, but things didn't go as planned."

"They hardly ever do," I said. "Glyptotheca"

11

is a word which here means "a place where sculpture is displayed," but I was more interested in unfolding the train. It had been constructed out of a single business card. All my associates in Stain'd-by-the-Sea had cards nowadays, printed with their names and areas of specialty. My eyes fell on the word "sculptor."

"Most of the statues were destroyed in a fire some time ago," Lost said. "Ornette was the one who smelled the smoke, which runs in the family too. By the time her uncles arrived to fight the fire, my daughter had managed to rouse the entire hotel and help the guests and staff to safety. Everyone was rescued—everyone but Alice."

I stopped looking at what was in my hands and stared into the sad eyes of Prosper Lost. I had always found the hotel where I had been living, and the man who ran it, to be shabby and uncomfortable. Not until now had I thought of either of them as damaged. "I'm sorry," I said. "I didn't know."

"I didn't tell you," Lost said, with his faint smile. "I suppose we all have our troubles, don't we, Snicket?"

"Mine are smaller than yours, Lost."

"I'm not so sure about that," Lost said quietly. "It seems to me we're in the same situation, both alone in the lobby."

"So you saw my chaperone go out?"

"Yes, just a minute ago."

"Did she tell you where she was going?"

"I'm afraid not."

"Did she say anything at all?"

Prosper Lost shifted slightly. It must have been tiring for him to stand up at the desk, but I don't think I'd ever seen him sit. "Actually," he said, "she told me that if she didn't return by tomorrow, I ought to make sure you were provided for."

"What?"

"She told me that if she didn't return—"

"I heard you, Lost. She said she wasn't

13

coming back." My chaperone had once told me she was leaving town, but our organization did not permit leaving apprentices unsupervised. I looked at the train again, fashioned out of a card that was designed for communication. But what is Ornette communicating, I asked myself. Myself couldn't answer, so I asked somebody else something else. "How long does the train stop at the station?"

"Oh, quite a while," Prosper said, with a glance at his watch. "The railway switches engines at Stain'd-by-the-Sea, and it takes a long time to load in all the passengers. It seems there are always more and more people who want to get out of town."

"Listen, Lost," I said. "If I don't return by tomorrow, will you do something for me?"

"What is it?"

"There's a book beside my bed," I said. "If I'm not back, please give it to the Bellerophon brothers."

"The taxi drivers?" he said. "All right, Snicket. If you say so. Although I'm surprised you're not bringing the book along. It seems to me that you always have a book with you."

"I do," I said, "but this book belongs to the library."

"The library was destroyed, Snicket. Don't you remember?"

"Of course I remember," I said, "but I still shouldn't take it with me. It's too bad, too. I'm only partway through."

"So it goes," Prosper Lost said, a little sadly. "There are some stories you never get to finish."

I nodded in agreement and I never saw him again. Outside, the night was colder than I would have guessed, but not colder than I like it. I headed toward the train station, thinking of the book. It was about a man who went to sleep one night, and when he woke up he was an insect. It was causing him a great deal of trouble. The streets were quiet and I went several blocks, all

15

the way to the town's last remaining department store, before I saw a single person.

Diceys was a tall building that looked like a neatly stacked pile of square windows, catching the starlight and winking it back at the sky. In each window was a mannequin dressed in Diceys clothes, posed with some item or other that the store had for sale. Diceys was closed at this time of night, but a few lights were still on inside, and the mannequins stood eerily looking down at the store's large entrance, a fancy door chained shut with a padlock as big as a suitcase. Struggling with the lock was S. Theodora Markson. Her efforts to unlock Diceys were fierce and required both her hands and occasionally a foot, and her bushy hair waved back and forth as she tried to wrestle her way into the store. From across the street she almost looked like an insect herself, as frantic and frightened as the man in the book. What happens next, I thought.

Finally, Theodora persuaded the door to

open and slipped inside Diceys. I waited just a few seconds before slipping after her. I didn't move too carefully. Anyone who struggles endlessly with a lock on a public street is not worried about being followed. There was a large, spiky metal object stuck in the lock. It was a skeleton key, but not a good one. A good skeleton key can open any lock at any time. A bad one can open some locks, some of the time, after much struggle. I looked at it, but only for a second, because I had seen it before. It was likely the only one in town. I left it where it was. I had no skeleton key as I stepped inside Diceys. I had only the clothes on my back, and a small folded paper train in my hand. My chaperone had something better. She had a secret.

CHAPTER TWO

Diceys was dark. I entered where perfume was sold, with glass bottles waiting on shelves like a laboratory with the mad scientist on vacation. I scanned the large room I was in. Nothing moved in it but a small light on a far wall. I made my way. The bottles watched me. I never have liked perfume. It always smells like someone's been hit by a truck full of flowers.

The light on the wall was over the elevator doors, indicating that the elevator was moving.

The light marked 4 turned on, and then the one marked 5. Theodora was going up. There was another elevator, but I couldn't risk taking it. I waited to see where it stopped. Then I'd take the stairs. I hoped it would stop soon. It stopped at 11.

The staircase was a fancy one, very wide, with banisters that were probably brass and carpeting that was probably red when the lights were on. With the lights off, the banister was just smudgy and the carpeting was dotted with light lint and dark stains. At each turn of the staircase was a sign telling me what they sold on the floor. The second floor sold shoes for men. The third floor sold shoes for women. The fourth floor also sold shoes for women. The fifth floor sold housewares, with radios and mixing bowls casting shapely shadows on the walls. The sixth floor sold toys, and I thought of a book for small children as I paused to catch my breath. A bear wanders a department store at night, looking for a button he has lost. He's caught by the night watchman. Diceys probably doesn't have a night watchman, I told myself. If they can't afford to polish the banisters, they can't afford to pay a man to watch over the place. They just lock the door and go home. In any case, you're not the one who broke in. Theodora broke in. You're just following her. So stop leaning against the banister and follow her.

The seventh floor sold formal clothing. The eighth sold casual clothing. The ninth sold children's clothing, and I remembered Theodora taking me there some weeks back, to be measured for new pants. It is embarrassing to be measured for new pants. The tenth floor sold the bright, shiny clothing people apparently enjoy wearing to play sports.

The eleventh floor sold uniforms. One of the advantages of the organization to which Theodora and I belonged was that there were no uniforms, unless you count a small tattoo on the ankle. I walked quietly between the racks of matching clothing hung up like flattened women and men, and wondered what Theodora was doing there. But she didn't seem to be there at all. Aisle after aisle of uniforms was empty. I looked this way and that. The uniforms shrugged back at me. Finally I reached the far end of the eleventh floor, where the windows looked down on the street. There was a mannequin dressed like a police officer in one window, and one dressed as a firefighter in the next. Then there was a uniformed nurse, and a cook, and a sailor, and then, standing in a window, there was a mannequin wearing nothing at all. At its feet were a pile of clothes I recognized as Theodora's. She had stood right there and changed her clothing, putting on whatever uniform had been worn by the mannequin. I did not like to think about it. I was at least relieved that Theodora's underwear was not in the pile, so she had not been completely naked in the window of a department store.

Out of the corner of my eye I saw a familiar light moving on a distant wall. The elevator was heading back down. "Why not?" I said to the bare mannequin. "She's gotten what she wanted."

The mannequin didn't say anything. I didn't want her job and she didn't want mine.

It was easier to go down the stairs, as it always is. In no time at all I was hurrying back past the perfume and out Diceys's front door. My chaperone hadn't thought to lock it back up again, but the skeleton key was gone. I could hear Theodora's footsteps and caught her distant silhouette as she rounded a corner, although I couldn't tell what she was wearing. She didn't look around. Why should she? She was in disguise and I was asleep in the Far East Suite.

Theodora took me past a diner called Hungry's, where my associate Jake Hix still occasionally slipped me a free meal, and Partial Foods, a grocery store where Hangfire had orchestrated some recent treachery. She walked quickly through the neighborhood and then past an enormous pen-shaped building, now abandoned, that once had been the home of my associate Cleo Knight, who was working on a formula for invisible ink that was Stain'd-by-the-Sea's best hope. I silently wished Cleo luck, and then found myself walking past Black Cat Coffee, a favorite haunt of Ellington Feint. I'd sat at the counter many times and watched the shiny machinery make small cups of strong coffee and loaves of fresh, warm bread. Had I known I'd never see it again, I might have taken a closer look. As it was, I hardly glanced inside the place. I knew Ellington Feint wasn't at Black Cat Coffee. The Officers Mitchum were putting her aboard the train. Soon she'd be in prison in the city, I thought, along with my sister. We walked a little farther, Theodora ahead and me following, until we were both where she wanted to be.

Stain'd Station was the busiest place I'd ever seen in town. The enormous room was thronging with people, and the noise of the crowd echoed up to the ceiling, which was lined with curved iron bars, like a black rainbow hanging in the loud air. Someone had lit torches that lined the walls, and by the flickering light I could see the train, twenty or thirty cars in length, at rest on one of the station's many tracks. Most of the train's cars were cargo cars, with INK INC. stamped on the sides and the tops open, to hold the ink extracted from octopi by enormous mechanized needles. But Ink Inc. was no longer a thriving business, and the octopi were scarcer and scarcer, so the cargo cars sat empty, ready to rattle through the fading town on tracks hardly used anymore. Behind the cargo cars were some passenger cars, decorated with wooden curlicues over the windows and old-fashioned railings bolted below and brightly painted designs everywhere else, and up front was a huge, tired engine, where people in black aprons hurried about with shovels and wheelbarrows, loading coal into the train's tender. Porters in bright blue jackets helped the passengers push their way through the crowd, and conductors in gray suits punched people's tickets with silver punchers clipped to their belts. Something was pinned to the lapels of their suits and jackets. I couldn't see what it was, but I could hear the echo of each puncher's *click* as it bounced off the ceilings, over and over again. Everyone seemed to be in a hurry to leave town.

Somewhere, I thought, is the car where they lock all of Stain'd-by-the-Sea's prisoners on their journey into the city. Somewhere there is Dashiell Qwerty and somewhere there is Ellington Feint, but you don't see them, do you, Snicket? You can't even find S. Theodora Markson, and you were supposed to be following her. With the black aprons, the blue jackets, and the gray suits, you don't even know what uniform to look for.

I found a ticket booth where a woman sat behind a window, reading a book I didn't like.

I didn't like the woman either. She was wearing an unfortunate smock with a little rip near the shoulder, right near a name tag printed with her name. I didn't need it. I remembered her well enough.

"Polly Partial," I said, and the owner of Partial Foods looked up and frowned at me.

"Total Stranger," she greeted me in return.

"We've met a number of times," I said, remembering that Ms. Partial had never been a reliable witness. "Why are you working here, instead of at your grocery store?"

"I have no more grocery store," she said sourly. "The place was closed due to lack of interest. Some thieves took all my honeydew melons, which really affected employee spirit."

"Well, at least your new job gives you time to read," I said, pointing at the book. "How are you enjoying that?"

"Not so well," she said.

"I've never liked that book."

"Oh, I think the book is very good," she said. "It's just that I was interrupted while I was reading it by some boy who keeps asking me questions."

"I'm sorry," I said, and I was a liar. "Is there room for one more passenger on that train?"

"*The Thistle of the Valley*?"

"Is that what the train is called?"

"Yes."

"When does it leave? Where does it stop?"

Polly Partial handed me a piece of paper printed on all sides with confusing times and locations. It looked like a herd of numbers having a square dance. I would rather have reread her book than Stain'd-by-the-Sea's confusing train schedule, but just barely. "I can't make head nor tail of this," I said.

She pointed to one of the squares on one of the charts. "*The Thistle of the Valley* leaves in two minutes from Track One," she said. "It winds through town, with brief stops at the post office, the museum, the library, and various downtown businesses, including Partial Foods and Ink Inc."

"Those places scarcely exist in this town anymore," I said.

"As you can see," she said, pointing to different squares, "all those stops have been canceled indefinitely."

"So then why did you mention them?" I asked her.

"It's standard policy," Polly Partial said, using a phrase which never means anything. "Unless there are special requests, *The Thistle of the Valley* makes no scheduled stops in town but travels across the sea and finally reaches the city before continuing on to various villages and tourist attractions."

"The sea doesn't exist anymore either," I reminded her. "There's only Offshore Island, a few remaining inkwells, and the Clusterous Forest."

"Don't tell me about the Clusterous Forest,"

Polly Partial said. "That area used to provide my store with fresh fish, before it became empty and lawless."

"I'm sorry about your business," I said.

"So am I," she replied, "but I'm not paid to listen to sympathetic comments. Do you want a ticket or not?"

"Yes, please," I said. "If possible I'd like to sit close to the prison car."

She blinked suspiciously at me. "We don't tell passengers if there are prisoners on board a train," she said. "That's standard policy."

"You don't have to tell me," I said. "I already know there are prisoners on board. I just want to sit close to them."

"I can't do that," she said. "There are only two compartments per train car, and the rear compartments have all been reserved."

"So the prison car is at the back of the train," I said. "Thank you very much."

Partial scowled and snatched back the schedule. "Do you want a ticket or not?"

"I don't have any money," I admitted.

"Then I suggest you scram and let me finish my book."

My hand was in my pocket, and I could feel the message Ornette had left for me, crinkly in my hand. "I need to get on that train," I said.

"No one gets aboard that train without a ticket identifying them as a passenger, or a thistle identifying them as an employee."

I pointed to the rip on her smock. "Where's your thistle?"

She quickly and badly tried to cover the rip with her hand. "A bird took it," she said. "I mean, it fell off."

"You're not a very good liar," I said.

"I never learned how," she said. "The grocery business is mostly an honest one."

"It can't be standard policy to give away

thistles," I said. "Perhaps I should report you to the railway company."

"They won't believe a child, a pest, and a nuisance."

I pointed at the book. "Give me a ticket or I'll give away the ending."

"You wouldn't dare," Polly Partial snarled. "Now scram. There's no ticket for you here."

"They find him guilty," I said. "The lawyer does his best at the trial, but the town finds Tom guilty just the same."

"You dirty rat," she sputtered. "I only had a few chapters to go."

I shrugged and walked away from the booth. I felt bad. It wasn't Polly Partial's fault that I didn't have money for a ticket, so I didn't really have a good reason to spoil the ending of the book. But I decided not to apologize for two reasons. The first was that I didn't feel like it. And the second was that someone had spotted me, someone who was striding toward me with a scowl that I'm sure matched my own.

It is not difficult to describe Sharon Haines, because we've all seen the likes of her plenty of times. Bad mothers are like old newspapers. No one has need of them, but they're everywhere, blowing around town. Sharon Haines was the mother of two children—a daughter named Lizzie, who had been kidnapped by Hangfire, and a son named Kellar, who had joined us to fight him. Sharon, on the other hand, had joined the Inhumane Society in a misguided effort to please the villain holding Lizzie captive. "Misguided" is a word which here means that it wasn't going to work, but even with her treachery revealed she continued to stride toward young people, barking orders and questions.

"Come over here, Snicket!" she barked. "What are you doing at Stain'd Station?"

"Being a child, a pest, and a nuisance," I said. "What are *you* doing here, Mrs. Haines?"

"I might ask you the same thing," she said haughtily.

"You already did," I said, and she gave me another scowl, although her heart wasn't in it. Her fingers fiddled nervously at her sides, one hand more nervously than the other, and her eyes were scanning the enormous room, back and forth like anxious pendulums. "I'm looking for someone too," I told her. "Wouldn't it be funny if we were both looking for the same person?"

Sharon gave me one more scowl and a gasp and then yet another scowl for good measure.

"Don't worry," I said. "We're not. You've already found the person I'm looking for. That's how you got your skeleton key back."

Sharon's hands raced to their pockets, but one pocket wasn't big enough. The skeleton key stuck out like a feather in a bad hat. It would be an easy caper to steal it like that. "You'd better get it back to Hangfire," I said. "I'm sure he has no idea you lent it to a friend."

"I'll thank you," she said sternly, "to stop interfering."

"Oh, you don't have to thank me, Mrs. Haines."

"Get out of here, young man. You have no idea what is going on."

"That's why I'm here," I said, but she gave me a little growl of frustration and stalked off. She came over to you, I told myself, and now she can't wait to walk away. A rude buzzer was ringing from someplace, and the station grew louder and busier. There were calls of "All aboard!" from the conductors, and passengers raced past me like I was nothing but an obstacle. A young woman stepped on my toe without apologizing, and my elbow got walloped by a suitcase carried by a man I probably should have looked at. The train was leaving shortly, and I wasn't on it. Think, Snicket. This is the train's only scheduled stop in town, and your only chance. How can you make your way onto that train?

"We have to get on that train!" exclaimed a voice near me, and a tall woman hurried through the crowd, followed by a porter who looked about my height and about my age. But it was the woman I recognized. Sally Murphy was once Stain'd-by-the-Sea's most celebrated actress and more recently had been among those who had fallen under the power of the Inhumane Society. Some time ago Ms. Murphy had put on a very convincing performance as the original owner of the statue of the Bombinating Beast, and at the moment appeared to be doing a very good imitation of someone very nervous.

"You," she said, very nervously.

I stood in her way and wouldn't budge. "Me," I agreed.

"I suppose you want me to thank you for your actions when we saw each other last."

"It is traditional to thank the person who

rescues you from drowning in the basement of an abandoned mansion," I agreed. "In fact, it might be said that you owe me a favor."

She tried to step around me this way and that. "Maybe I can buy you an ice cream cone sometime," she said quickly.

I kept on not budging. "That's not what I want."

"All children want ice cream."

"What I want is to get aboard that train," I told her.

"It's a very popular night to leave town."

"So I've noticed," I said, watching Sharon Haines disappear into the crowd. "Can you tell me why you're leaving?"

Sally Murphy took a quick look at her porter. "Please don't ask me that."

"If you're doing more work for the Inhumane Society," I said, "then you'll need to explain yourself to the police."

The actress looked wildly around her, like a

field mouse in the shadow of a hawk. Even Sally Murphy's porter looked a bit frightened. "Not so loud!" Sally hissed to me. "I'll thank you to stop interfering."

"Why does everyone keep wanting to thank me for the same thing?" I asked, but the porter stopped the actress from answering my question.

"We'd best be getting on, ma'am," the porter said. "We don't want to miss the train."

"*I* don't want to miss it," Sally Murphy corrected, and I took a better look at the person she was speaking to. The porter had wide eyes and a mustache that quivered. It was a striking mustache, I noticed—so perfectly square that it looked more like a piece of paper. Of course, I thought, a person my age with a mustache was already striking. The porter's hair was striking too, with hairpins poking out here and there all porcupiney, and the uniform was the right one—a bright blue jacket with a thistle on the lapel—but fit all wrong. Uniform, I thought.

Disguise. But it certainly wasn't my chaperone I was looking at. There weren't enough hairpins in the world to tame the mane of S. Theodora Markson.

"Tell me," I said to the actress, "are you helping Hangfire or escaping him?"

Sally Murphy looked down at me, and I saw one tear in her eye, slow and bright, looking down at me too. "I'll never escape from Hangfire," she said quietly, "but perhaps an actress can manage the most important performance of her life. Come now, porter."

"Yes, ma'am," the porter said, and then finally I budged. I budged to the left and Ms. Murphy and the porter budged over to where a conductor was standing. Ornette's folded sculpture crinkled in my pocket again. A paper train, I thought. Sharon Haines. Sally Murphy. S. Theodora Markson. I knew there was a mystery here, but the mystery mystified me.

With a *click!*, the conductor punched the

actress's ticket, and Sally Murphy and the porter walked toward *The Thistle of the Valley*. "Excuse me," I said to the conductor, quickly and desperately. "I need to get on that train, but I'm afraid I don't have a ticket."

"Then you're out of luck," the conductor said. "That's standard policy."

"Pretty please?" I asked, which never works, and sure enough the conductor shook his head.

"Another train will come along before too long, sonny boy," he said.

"I need to be on tonight's train," said sonny boy.

"Why tonight?"

"I'm not sure," I admitted, and he gave me the look adults give to children they call sonny boy. I frowned back at him, but it didn't help. Sally Murphy disappeared into the train, and I watched her porter follow with the bags. He's right, Snicket. The conductor is right. You're out of luck.

The buzzer buzzed again, and the conductors began to shut the doors of the train. *The Thistle of the Valley* blew its whistle, loud and bright like an adventure was starting. The heavy wheels began to move, a clackety racket that echoed everywhere, first slowly and then quicker and quicker. The engine grumbled its way out of view, then the tender and then the cargo cars, one by one, lonely without the ink that ought to have been in them. Next came the passenger cars, with silhouettes of passengers here and there in the windows, too quick and distant to recognize. I tried to recognize them anyway as they went past, actors or chaperones, friends or foes, strangers or people pretending to be strangers. But by now the train was moving too quickly for me to see anything more than a few pale faces behind the blank glass, as if *The Thistle of the Valley* were full of ghosts. I could see the last car approaching, and then I saw it pass, locked tight so the prisoners couldn't escape, although it felt like they were escaping anyway, out of my sight and out of my reach. The last of the train left Stain'd Station like sand through my fingers, and I just stood there watching, helpless and useless. The mystery is leaving, Snicket. Your investigation is escaping, and now you're all alone.

The station took a while to settle down, and I stood for a moment with my hands in my pockets, one clenching a paper train and the other clenching nothing. I didn't want to give up, so I tried to guess what to do next. I guessed and then I kept guessing and then I couldn't guess and then I gave up. Trudging out of the station, however, turned out to be the right guess after all, because a solution was stopped just at the curb, honking its horn and calling my name.

"Is that you, Snicket?"

I smiled. "Is that you, Pip and Squeak?"

The boy at the wheel smiled, and his brother crawled up from his position at the brake pedal so they could both hand me cards through the taxi's open window. The cards told me what I already knew. Bouvard and Pecuchet Bellerophon, better known as Pip and Squeak, provided discreet transportation, a phrase which meant they drove the only taxi left in Stain'd-by-the-Sea whenever their father was sick or couldn't do it for some other reason, which was almost all the time and always. They weren't quite tall enough to drive by themselves, but with Pip steering and Squeak on the pedals, they'd gotten me out of a few tight spots after getting me into them more or less on time.

I hurried into the back of the cab. "I need you two on a tail job."

"Neat," Squeak said, in the voice that gave him his nickname. "Since we started driving this taxi, I've been waiting for someone to say 'follow that car.'"

"It's not a car I want you to follow," I said. "It's a train."

"Follow a train?" Pip repeated with a laugh. "That's hardly a tail job. It runs on tracks, doesn't it? Why do we need to follow a train when we already know where it goes?"

"I need you to take me to where it goes before it gets there," I said.

"So instead of 'follow that car' it's 'precede that train'?" Squeak asked, sliding down to his pedal spot. He sounded a little disappointed.

"I need to get onto *The Thistle of the Valley*," I said, "but I couldn't manage it here."

Pip frowned. "But there's nowhere else you can get on board. They canceled all the old stops in town."

"That's why I need you to take me to Partial Foods," I said. "The back entrance, off the alley, where the train tracks are."

"Didn't you hear us, Snicket?" Pip asked. "*The Thistle of the Valley* doesn't stop there or anyplace else."

"I heard you."

Pip put the car in gear. "I hope you're not going to do anything foolish."

"I hope you're not hoping too hard," I said. Squeak hit the gas and we pulled away from Stain'd Station and took a shortcut toward our destination. I heard the train whistle blow again, and thought of Theodora's phony snores. Breathe and keep still, I told myself, thinking of the foolish thing in my immediate future.

"It's been a busy night," Squeak said, as we rounded the corner.

"I was supposed to be in bed early," I said.

Pip grinned at me in the rearview mirror. "That's always the way, isn't it? The most interesting things happen when we're supposed to be in bed. What were you doing at Stain'd Station, anyway?"

"Official business," I said.

"I guess we should keep all our actions quiet," Squeak said. "That way Hangfire won't catch on."

"We hope," Pip said.

"We hope," I agreed, but I didn't feel agreeable. I wondered what the Bellerophons were up to. And Ornette, I thought. And Theodora, and Sally Murphy and her strange porter. And my sister, and a thousand other people I might not see again. Not after what I was about to do. I looked out at the night, and the taxi turned left and swung into the shadow of Ink Inc., the pen-shaped tower making the dark even darker just where we were.

"Snicket," Squeak said, braking and breaking the silence, "how about you give us a tip like you do?"

I had a system with the Bellerophon brothers, recommending books in exchange for their services. It's a system I wish were used more widely in the world. "Have you read a book called *The Turn of the Screw*?" I asked.

Pip pointed his thumb at the hood of the taxi. "We get enough hardware in our ordinary lives," he said.

"It's not about hardware," I told him. "It's about a babysitter and some ghosts. It's difficult but it's spooky, and speaking of which, stop here, will you?"

The Bellerophons stopped their taxi, and I peered out at the loading dock of Partial Foods. It was empty and eerie, with a crumbling cement ramp and the back door of the grocery store, locked now and probably forever. I could see a discarded apple core, sad and mushy in a clump of weeds, and the torn wrapper of a long-gone candy bar, balled up and forgotten near the train tracks.

"You never told us the whole story of what happened here, with all those stolen honeydew melons," Pip reminded me, referring to recent events chronicled in a report that is not recommended for the general public.

"True," I admitted.

"The train won't stop here," Squeak said to me. "It'll just race on by."

"I know it," I replied.

Pip turned around to look at me. "Do we have to ask again about doing something foolish?"

"No," I said. "You definitely don't have to ask."

"Maybe that's the wrong question," Squeak said, looking at the strange, bare place where he and his brother had taken me. "Maybe the right question is, do you really want to be here?"

I thought of all the places I wanted to be, not as difficult and not as spooky. I stepped out of the car and deeper into a mystery of which I couldn't make head nor tail, and I answered the question the best I could.

"No," I said, "I don't want to be here," and I thanked them for taking me there and sent them on their way.

CHAPTER THREE

The night kept me in its shadows as I waited by Partial Foods and listened for the train. I kept breathing and I kept still. From down the alley came the scufflings of some animal that lurked around at night. Most such animals won't bother you, but their noises are still unnerving. I sat, unnerved, and tried to get un-unnerved. It's just nature, I told myself. Nature's not interested in you, Snicket. I was wrong about that too.

The train whistle blew and the clatter and

hiss of the engine grew louder, frightening whatever was behind the shack to scuffle off else-
where. Soon the train would pass where I was
waiting, moving with great speed and a greater
clanging. It wouldn't stop. It wouldn't stop here
or anyplace else. It would just rush by, billowing
air into my face as it headed out of town, into the
valley where the ocean once thrived, and toward
the city, carrying passengers and prisoners and
perhaps a stowaway. I stood up. "Stowaway" is a
word for a person hiding on a ship, so they can
travel without paying. Of course, I thought to
myself, it doesn't have to be a ship. It couldn't
be a ship anyway, Snicket. Not in Stain'd-by-the-
Sea. There's nowhere to sail a ship. There's still
a train, though. The train is called *The Thistle of
the Valley* and it's racing toward you now. First the
engine will appear, and then the tender, brim-
ming with coal, and then a long line of cargo
cars marked with the name of the town's greatest
industry, now almost completely gone. And the

end of the train will appear, moving as quickly as anything, a few passenger cars brightly painted and decorated with old-fashioned railings.

And you, I thought to myself, are going to grab on to one of those railings as the train goes past, and then try to open one of the windows and get inside while the train barrels through the countryside.

The engine raced by me, its headlight like an angry eye, its steam fading into the purple sky, and the noise everywhere in the air.

Nothing will happen to you, I told myself. You've already had a very interesting childhood, Lemony Snicket. At a very young age you were recruited into a secret organization. When you were six you were taken deep into the forest for nine days of archery training. In the evenings you caught and roasted wild pheasant, and at night you could hear the wolves gnawing on the bones as you shivered in your tent. Everything since then has been anticlimactic, a word which here means "nowhere near as exciting." It will be very boring, in fact, when you leap onto the train as it rattles its way out of Stain'd-by-the-Sea and then crawl your way inside. Very dull indeed, Snicket.

The cargo cars began to go by with great *swoosh*es, one after the other.

Look, everybody has a turn, Snicket. Giacomo Casanova had a turn. Marcel Duchamp had a turn. Beverly Cleary had a turn. People have done difficult things for more or less noble reasons. Your turn now.

I stepped closer. The railings were skinny metal bars, bolted here and there to the side of the train. They were just for decoration. There was no way of knowing how much weight they might hold. Below them were three small grooves in the metal, like three footprints on each car of the train. You might be able to balance your feet on these grooves and you might not. *Swoosh, swoosh, swoosh.* I leaned down and cast my eyes toward the last cars of the train. They were almost there. In a moment it would be time to jump. My palms were sweaty and I wiped them on my pants and they were sweaty again in seconds. Here it comes, I thought. It is coming quickly, so you do not have time to be scared, Snicket. Not scared, not now.

"Get scared later," I said out loud, and I leapt toward the speeding train. If you're wondering what it's like to cling to a decorative railing on the side of a moving railway car, don't. But I didn't have to wonder what it was like because I learned immediately it was terrible. It was as terrible as it was loud, and it was deafening. From the moment my hands touched the metal railing and grasped it tightly, my ears were full of noise. There was the noise of the wheels of the train, rough and clattery like wild teeth on the tracks, and there was the sound of complaining metal as the railing heaved with my weight. And there was another sound, throaty

and trembly. I did not know what it was. I did
not care. My every thought was focused on keeping my hands on the railing even as the train
rocked back and forth and the sweat on my
palms made the whole plan slippery. My face
was pressed against a bright red design. My feet
found the topmost groove and slipped out of it,
and then the middle groove and slipped out of
it, and then the bottommost groove and slipped
out of it, so my feet struggled and dangled below
me, just inches from the racing wheels. The railing kept complaining. It shook in my hands like
it wanted to leave. I didn't blame it. It was so difficult to hold on that it was tempting to let go. I
held on, though. Dear Kit, went another imaginary letter to my sister. I write to you from outside a roaring train, where I am about to lose my
life. All I can see is a design the color of those
rain boots they used to make you wear. I send
best wishes and warm personal regards.

The train rounded a curve, and without any-where for my feet to go, I found my body thrown hard against the side of the train, over and over again, like a swinging door. It hurt every time in a new place. First it was my knee and then it was my chin and then my shoulder and then my nose and then it was my knee again and then I lost track. I was tired of looking at the design and tilted my head to try and see where the window was. It was above me. It was not open, of course. Why should it be open? No one was around to make this easier for me. The train rattled again and my body slammed again against the side. The metal complained more and the trembly sound grew louder. I looked up at the window again. I would have to climb up the shaking, smooth wall of the train and hope there was a crack in the window somewhere to slip through. Very easy, if I were a spider.

The railing told me what it thought of this

plan by spitting out a bolt with a terrible creak. It was not the only bolt holding the railing to the train, but it was one of them and it was gone. The railing complained louder and began to shake against my hands. The other sound grew louder too. It was me, I realized. I'd been crying out since I leapt onto the train. I was crying out because I was going to die.

But I didn't die, of course. Not then. I let go of the railing with one arm and raised my fist to bang against the window of the train. My arm felt weak as it swung upward, and the knock against the glass was nowhere near as loud as I wanted it to be. I stopped to hold on again and let the train throw me against the side of the car several more times. It hurt. The railing curved terribly away from the train, like a tree struggling in a hurricane, and another bolt sprang loose and fell into the night. Things like that make the world seem unfair, I thought to myself, and heaved my arm up again and banged on the window. The railing bent further, and I could feel the breath of the spinning wheels on my feet. One more inch and the wheels would eat me alive. My fist kept knocking. A terrible scrape of metal came from where the bolts had escaped. I got tired of looking at the bright red design. I did not want it to be the last thing I saw, so I closed my eyes, and I knocked and knocked and felt my mouth go raw with the noise I was making.

Something slid above me. I tried to knock again and only hit air. I heard other sounds I could not hear over the train. And then like a miracle something grabbed my arm as I was giving up. I heard more sounds and then I was heaved, slowly, slowly, out of my predicament. I kept my eyes closed. My aching body scraped against something and then fell in a heap. Someone stood over the heap. I blinked at the carpet and tried to sit up. It didn't work as well as I would have liked. The carpet was a faded sort of ugly. I was not bleeding and I was not broken, but it took all the strength I had just to raise my head. All I saw were the shoes of whoever had rescued me. It surprised me that I recognized them. They were ordinary brown shoes, a little scuffy. But friends know more about one another than they might think.

"What's the news, Moxie?" I asked, when I was in a condition to ask anything.

Moxie Mallahan, Stain'd-by-the-Sea's last journalist and one of my most loyal associates, knelt down beside me. The hat she usually wore lay on the floor next to me, with a few scattered business cards stating her name and occupation. I could tell she had a thousand questions, but she only asked me one. "What are you doing here?"

"Recuperating," I told her. "I was hanging on the outside of this train."

"You ever hear of buying a ticket?"

"It's an unexpected journey," I said. "How did you manage to pull me up here?"

"You don't lug around a typewriter for years without getting a few muscles," she said.

She picked up her hat, and I managed to sit up and look at my surroundings. It was an ordinary train compartment, about the size of the bedroom given the least-favorite child. Two walls had two benches, facing each other like silent strangers, and there was a wooden door, closed and tired, that probably led to a corridor outside. Underneath the window, still open and full of rushing scenery, was a small, scuffed table attached to the wall. Above each bench was a rack for luggage, but the only luggage I could see was the case where Moxie kept her new typewriter, and a small parcel wrapped in newspaper and string.

"What are you doing here?" I said.

Moxie shook her head and grinned. "Only Lemony Snicket," she said, "would hang off the outside of a train and then ask a passenger what they were doing there. A stunt like that could have killed you."

"That did occur to me," I admitted. "But it seemed important to be on this very train on this very night. My chaperone went to the trouble of stealing herself a disguise just to get aboard."

Moxie's eyes widened. "Theodora's here?"

I nodded. "And she's not the only one. Sally Murphy boarded *The Thistle of the Valley* moments before it departed."

Moxie looked from me to her typewriter case, hungry to take notes. "Do you think she's still working with Hangfire?"

"I don't know," I told her. "She said something about an actress giving the performance of a lifetime. And there's something else."

"What is it?"

I reached into my pocket and drew out the paper train. By now it was quite crumpled, but you could still see how cleverly it was constructed.

"Ornette Lost," Moxie said. "She can make anything out of a scrap of paper."

"She has quite a few impressive skills," I said, thinking of what Prosper Lost had told me about the fire. "She made this out of one of her cards and left it for me at the Lost Arms. It's a message. She was telling me something about this train."

Moxie glanced quickly at her typewriter again. "Telling you what?"

"You know perfectly well what," I said. "That's why you keep looking over at that parcel. You might as well fetch it, along with your typewriter, so you can take notes while you tell me what's going on."

"Are you sure I should tell you? You're the one who said we should work separately, Snicket. I haven't even told Kellar Haines what I'm doing tonight, and he's still living with my father and me at the lighthouse. Every night he stares at that photograph of his sister he showed us. He's

63

really itching to defeat Hangfire and rescue Lizzie."

"I think we all have that itch," I said. "Is that why you're on this train with that mysterious package?"

Moxie sighed and reached up to the luggage rack. "I guess I'm not a very good secret-keeper," she said, taking down the two items.

"You're a very good journalist," I said, "which is the opposite of secret-keeping. I bet you're here following a story."

She shook her head and put down the typewriter case on one of the benches. The parcel she kept in her hands. "'Following' isn't the right word," she said. "'Following' means that you're trailing behind somebody, and I'm trailing ahead. What's the word for that, Snicket?"

I leaned against the other bench. Even that hurt. "Preceding," I said.

"Well," she said, "then I'm on this train

preceding a very important person, who will accompany me to the city."

I looked out the compartment window, where I could see the town's traffic lights, flickering in the darkness as they pretended there was still traffic on the vanishing streets. It was a strange sight. I never got used to it in all my time in Stain'd-by-the-Sea. *"The Thistle of the Valley* won't stop again in town," I said. "Nowadays the train travels across the sea to the city before continuing on to various villages and tourist attractions. A retired grocer told me that herself."

"Usually that's true," Moxie agreed, "but not tonight."

"Not tonight," I repeated, and then I asked her the question found on the cover of this book. It was the wrong question, and it was wrong again later, when Hangfire asked it of me. The right question was "Where had the train been before it stopped at Stain'd-by-the-Sea?" but not until it was too late did I think to ask it.

"Take a guess," she said.

"The lawyer does his best at the trial, but the town finds Tom guilty just the same."

Moxie gave me the frown my guess deserved. "Tonight the train is making an extra stop," she said, "and a very important passenger is getting on."

"Is that so?" I asked.

"That is so," Moxie replied. Her eyes sparkled with excitement, and the parcel crumpled a little in her jittery hand. I noticed the scar on her arm. A knife wound had made the scar during a time of danger, and it would likely never fade completely. It was a mark in her skin that would last forever, even if it didn't hurt anymore. But Moxie wasn't worried about getting hurt. She grinned at me as she loosened the string around the package so she could unfold the newspaper a little and show me what was inside.

"Who is this important passenger?" I asked, but I almost forgot the question as soon as it was out of my mouth. I was looking at something. The parted newspapers revealed a face to me, the fierce and angry face of an animal. It looked a little like a sea horse and a lot like a monster. The monster was a source of mystery and terror in ancient myths, and the statue of the monster was a source of mystery and terror to me since I had arrived in Stain'd-by-the-Sea to investigate its disappearance. And now here it was, in a train compartment. I stared and stared at the item in my associate's hands, and knew the answer to my question even as Moxie said it.

"Hangfire," she said, but I kept staring at the Bombinating Beast.

CHAPTER FOUR

"Was that a knock on the door?" Moxie asked me.

I looked up impatiently from the Bombinating Beast. "Was *what* a knock on the door?"

Moxie was wise to ignore me, and got up to slide shut the window, making it considerably quieter. Stain'd-by-the-Sea rattled by softer in the dark, and we listened until it happened again. It was a knock on the door. We looked across the compartment. The door had a little latch that worked a little lock, but Moxie hadn't thought to lock the door, and neither had I.

The knock knocked again. I looked at Moxie and she looked at me. "Yes?" she called out.

"Conductor," said a woman's voice. It wasn't Theodora's. This doesn't mean I didn't recognize it.

"I'm also a conductor," said another voice. This one was a man. "We're here to check everyone's tickets."

"Just a moment," Moxie answered, and gave me a panicked look.

"Let them in," I whispered to her.

"But you don't have a ticket," she whispered back, quickly tying the parcel shut again. "That looks suspicious."

"Not as suspicious as standing on the other side of the door whispering," I told her, and she put the Bombinating Beast back on the shelf and opened the door.

The woman and the man came in. She was

old enough to be my mother and he was old enough to be my father, but neither of them were either of them. Moxie was quick to take her ticket out of her pocket, and then both conductors turned to me. The train rounded a slight corner, tilting the compartment for a second as they looked. People in our organization have been taught how not to seem surprised, which is as important a part of disguising yourself as stealing a uniform, but I could see that this woman and this man had not learned this skill very well. They stared at me like toddlers at a clown.

"Yes, it's me," I told them.

"I should introduce myself, too," Moxie said quickly, and reached down to the floor to hand one of her cards to each of them. "I'm a journalist, and this gentleman is an associate of mine."

"*Moxie Mallahan*," the woman read out loud. "*The News*."

"What's the news?" the man said.

"The news is that I lost my ticket," I said, "but Ms. Mallahan can vouch for me."

"But this is just a business card," the woman said.

"You can get anything printed on a card like this," the man said. "It's the easiest disguise in the world."

"Putting on a uniform might be easier," I said.

Both adults gasped, and then remembered that they weren't supposed to gasp in such situations. "We are real live train conductors," the man said, which is no way to convince someone you are a real live train conductor.

"And what real live train conductors do," the woman said, "is check everyone's tickets. Do you have one?"

"Of course I have a ticket."

The man sighed and put his hands on his hips, a gesture I'm sure you recognize from all the times you lied badly to an adult. "Well, where is it?"

"I ate it," I said. "It reminded me of break-fasts I've had at the Hemlock Tearoom and Sta-tionery Shop. Those are pretty awful."

She blinked and the man blinked with her. Moxie blinked too, and gave me a look that was both furtive and incredulous, words which mean she couldn't believe I was saying such things.

"Particularly the tea," I couldn't help adding.

"That's enough out of you, sonny," the man said.

"I'm not your son," I said, "although I sup-pose people might think so, if they saw us together. Perhaps we should ask Ms. Mallahan what she thinks. As a reporter, she'd be most interested in what is going on. Wouldn't you, Moxie?"

Moxie grasped the handle of her typewriter case. She still looked furtive and incredulous, but now she also looked eager and investigative and full of questions. "I most certainly would," she said, but the two adults backed away from her typewriter as if it were a powerful weapon, which in some ways it is. The man fiddled with the latch on the door, but the door was already unlocked, so he managed to lock it again, making it difficult to open, rather than unlock it, making it easy, and the woman was meanwhile turning the knob of the door this way and that. It was an awkward dance, made more awkward by the silence in the compartment. Finally the man managed to unlock the door and the woman managed to open it and the two adults walked through, first simultaneously, a word which here means they tried to walk through the door at the same time and got tangled up, and then ridiculously, a word which here means that the man stepped through the door and closed it behind him, catching it on the woman's fingers, and she shrieked and the door opened again and she stepped through after him and the door shut again and at last they were gone. Moxie stared after them like they were a circus leaving town.

"What was *that*?" she asked.

"*That*," I said, "was a man named Gifford and a woman named Ghede. They're both members of my organization."

"V.F.D.?" she said in astonishment.

"Not so loud, Moxie."

"Sorry. But they're like you?"

"Gifford and Ghede are not at all like me."

"What do you mean?"

"Not long ago they spiked my tea with laudanum," I said.

"Why would members of your own organization try to knock you unconscious with a dangerous chemical?"

"Why would my own chaperone break into a department store and steal a uniform?" I asked her back. "Why would Sharon Haines be lurking around Stain'd Station? Why would a celebrated actress board *The Thistle of the Valley* with a suspicious-looking porter? And why would my prime associate be on board the same train with

75

the Bombinating Beast wrapped up in newspaper and string without my knowing what she was up to?"

"Do you really think of me as your prime associate?"

"That is hardly the point."

"I'm sorry I didn't tell you about this," she said, "but you're the one who said we should work in the shadows and communicate as quietly as possible."

"That was before I had an early bedtime, followed my chaperone to Diceys to steal a uniform, and almost fell off a speeding train."

Moxie put a gentle hand on my shoulder. "You've been through a rough scrape, haven't you? You need something restorative. Let me see what Jake Hix fixed up."

She opened the typewriter case with a *click*. It was a new typewriter—Hangfire had confiscated her old one—and the new case had more room in it, enough space for a lumpy paper sack.

My stomach told the sack to hurry up. After my experience on the railing, a Hix meal would hit the spot.

"*The Thistle of the Valley* used to have a grand Café Car," Moxie said, "with poppy seed bagels and almond pound cake and verbena tea and root beer floats in frosted glasses. But as the town faded away, the Café Car was replaced by a Café Compartment, but it's just coffee and tired fruit served on the honor system. So I asked Jake if he'd whip up a few things for the journey."

Sure enough, a few things emerged from the bag. Moxie laid them on the bench one by one. There were two little glass bottles, narrow at the top and wide on the bottom, and a big hunk of what smelled like gingerbread, and a paper box with a folded lid that opened to reveal a small tomato salad. I knew the tomatoes were from the garden Jake tended with his sweetheart, Cleo Knight, a brilliant chemist and another associate of mine. The last item was wrapped up in wax paper and looked for a moment like a small stack of pages, as if Jake had given Moxie the manuscript for a miniature book.

"Jake has started naming his sandwiches," she told me. "This is the Highsmith. It's roasted peppers, apricots, and walnuts, with Stilton cheese and some kind of lettuce I'm forgetting. It's either endive or escarole."

"That's the second most interesting thing you've unwrapped this evening," I said, and took half. "Now why don't you show me the first again?"

Moxie took down the parcel and unwrapped it as I took the first bite. Jake Hix had never let me down before, and he still hadn't. It was escarole and I couldn't eat it fast enough.

"It's not what you think it is," she said, when I could see its angry face again. The Bombinating Beast stared at me with its empty eyes and bared its teeth at me—small, straight, sharp teeth that clung to my nightmares. "It's not a statue of a monster."

"It must be more than that, if Hangfire wants it," I said, with my mouth full. "Now that we have the Bombinating Beast, maybe we can finally figure out its secret."

"You misunderstood," Moxie said. "Take it and you'll see."

I took it and I saw. As soon as I hefted the statue into my hands I could tell it was wrong. It was far too light, like a box with nothing in it, instead of a strange item heavy with sinister secrets. I looked more closely and saw that it wasn't carved out of wood, or out of anything at all. I was holding something fashioned from stiff black cardboard, folded intricately into the shape of the Bombinating Beast.

"Ornette Lost," I said.

Moxie nodded. "I told you she could make anything out of a scrap of paper," she said, "although in this case it's black cardboard, from the laudanum boxes at Wade Academy. Ornette came over to the lighthouse to look at all the beast souvenirs we have lying around, and she finished putting this together late last night." She took a bite of tomato salad and gave me a wicked grin. "I'm going to fool Hangfire," she said. "I managed to get a message to him at Offshore Island this morning telling him that the Bombinating Beast could be delivered to him if he came on board *The Thistle of the Valley* tonight."

"Does he know you're doing the delivering?"

"Of course not," Moxie said. "He would never trust me. I escaped from Wade Academy, and he knows I'm a member of the press. I just told him which compartment I had reserved. He took the bait, Snicket. As soon as *The Thistle of the Valley* started its journey, the conductors announced an unscheduled stop at Offshore

Island. It's got to be Hangfire, coming aboard to meet me."

"But what will you do when he's here?" I asked, after a sip of fizzy water. "Ornette's creation looks very much like the real statue, but once it's in Hangfire's hands he'll know it's a fake."

"Once Hangfire comes aboard," Moxie said, "he'll be caught like a rat in a trap. *The Thistle of the Valley* won't stop again until it reaches the city, where all the prisoners on board will be brought to trial. I have all our notes on what Hangfire's been doing in this town. Once the authorities read my report, they'll arrest Hangfire, and Dashiell Qwerty will go free."

"You think Hangfire's going to walk onto this train at Offshore Island, and end up in the hands of the authorities?" I asked doubtfully, my mouth busy with the last bite of Highsmith. "He seems far too clever for that."

"He's too greedy to be too clever," Moxie said. "He framed Dashiell Qwerty. He captured all those children and is holding them captive at Wade Academy. He stole equipment from the aquarium, and honeydew melons from Partial Foods. Everything's ready for his terrible scheme, whatever it may be. All he needs is the statue of the Bombinating Beast. If he thinks it's here on the train, he'll come aboard tonight to get his hands on it."

Moxie took a sip of fizzy water and then unwrapped the gingerbread and gave me a piece. It was sweet, but not too sweet, like all of my favorite desserts and people. We ate in silence for a moment, and then Moxie licked her fingers and looked at me.

"So?" she said.

"So what?"

"So what do you think, Snicket? This will be the greatest journalistic triumph in the history of Stain'd-by-the-Sea. I only wish my mother were here to see it."

Moxie's mother, I knew, was a reporter who had left Stain'd-by-the-Sea some time ago, and Moxie had not heard any word from her. "I'm sure she'll hear about it," I said, though I was not sure at all.

Moxie reached over and tapped on the window. Outside I could see the dark landscape slipping beneath us as the train's route rose onto a bridge. Before the sea had been drained away, the bridge had water beneath it, and I thought I saw something flicker where the water had once been, or two somethings, really, two little round lights. But then they were gone. "This bridge leads to Offshore Island," Moxie said. "We'll be stopping at Wade Academy any moment. I told Hangfire to come alone, which means the Inhumane Society won't be able to help him. All I have to do is lie low for a few more minutes so nobody knows I'm on board until the train starts up again. Then Hangfire will be caught at last, and you'll be here to witness it. After all this time, we may finally be in the penultimate chapter of Hangfire's treachery."

"Penultimate is a word I've always liked," I said.

"You like the word," she said, "but not the plan."

"You're right. I don't like it."

"Why not?"

"You're trying to lure Hangfire aboard," I said. "Usually it's Hangfire who does the luring."

"Then maybe this time Hangfire will lose, and V.F.D. will win."

"I hope so," I said, "but villainy is like a bad guest. If it accepts your invitation, it leaves its terrible mess everywhere you look."

Moxie didn't have anything to say to that, and I didn't have anything to say to her not having anything to say. But someone else spoke up.

It was the voice of a man, raised in anger but muffled by walls. We looked across the compartment. Another voice replied, a woman or perhaps a girl, just as angry and just as muffled. It was an argument, loud but impossible to hear.

"That's the prison car," Moxie said, with a nod at the wall. "We're listening to something one of the prisoners is saying."

"No, we're not," I said, and picked up the bottle of fizzy water. "But we can in a minute."

I was thirsty, which I regret. If I hadn't been thirsty, I might have emptied the bottle by pouring it out the window. Instead, I drank the rest of the water and then laid the bottle against the far wall. An empty bottle or glass is a decent way to hear what is going on on the other side of the wall. A stethoscope would have been better, and of course the best way to hear what is happening in the next room is to walk into it and participate in the conversation. The empty bottle will have to do, I told myself, even though the voices

I heard kept fading in and out, like the people talking were ghosts already.

"…before someone else sees you," the voice was saying, when I pressed my ear against the bottom of the bottle. "I know what I'm doing, Theodora, and I can't have you mucking it up."

You cannot work as closely as I'd worked with a librarian like Dashiell Qwerty without recognizing his deep voice, steady and precise. Now it sounded unsteady and imprecise. I didn't like it. "I'm here to rescue you, Qwerty," my chaperone replied. "Getting you out of this cell is a good way to get high marks on my evaluation." Theodora was using a brash, rude voice I never liked to hear, even from the next train car.

She said something else, in a voice that was much calmer, but I couldn't hear what it was, just the exasperated sigh at the end.

"It's not proper," Qwerty said, "to discuss this in front of—"

"Don't talk to me of proper," Theodora said.

"I know my progress in this town has been monitored, and I know you've been monitoring it." She lowered her voice again, or was interrupted. I leaned closer, but it was just a murmur over the noise of the train.

"You've done a lousy job," Qwerty said, "but that won't matter, Markson. Once I get to the city, I can tell the others the truth about…" The end of the sentence was swallowed up.

Someone murmured and then Theodora spoke up. "What about my evaluation?"

"Be sensible, Markson."

"I am sensible, Qwerty. You and all your library books," and something rattled and I missed it.

Qwerty sighed. "The library is gone," I heard him admit, "and the book is destroyed. Villainy can win against one library, but not against an organization of readers. I have the information that can stop Hangfire."

More murmuring, more rattling. "…a good

evaluation," Theodora finished, in the same voice she'd used to make me go to bed early.

"You haven't earned a good evaluation," Qwerty said sharply.

"I'll tell you what I've earned," Theodora said, and then she said something else I couldn't hear, in the quiet tone. Qwerty heard it, though. The librarian now sounded less steady and precise and more frightened and anxious, or perhaps I was hearing my own fright and anxiety.

"What are you doing?" he cried, and then there was a loud, shattering noise that sounded so close I thought the bottle had broken against my ear. Qwerty screamed, a wild, loud sound he never would have allowed in his library, and then I don't know exactly what happened next because I dropped the bottle.

"What is it?" Moxie asked me. "What's going on?"

"Let's find out," I said, moving to the door.

"I can't," Moxie said. "I need to lie low, remember?"

I remembered and said so, then hurried out of the compartment and found myself in a narrow corridor, clattering with the noise of the train and full of nobody but me. At either end were sliding doors to the neighboring train cars, and above me were little star-shaped lights set in the sad ceiling. One wall was lined with the doors to the two compartments, and the other with wide, clear windows looking outside. The scenery was slowing, and I felt the clattering of the wheels get slower and slower on the bridge beneath me. *The Thistle of the Valley* was making its unscheduled stop.

I rushed to the end of the corridor, each footstep shaky on the shifting floor, and reached a set of sliding glass doors that separated our train car from the next. I expected the sliding doors to be locked, and perhaps they had been. But now the doors were wide open. Stain'd-by-the-Sea's two police officers, Mimi and Harvey Mitchum, were standing in the prison car, a darker, sterner version of the passenger cars. There were two cells, labeled CELL ONE and CELL TWO, each with a door that looked heavy and difficult to open, but Harvey had opened one, and was now staring grimly into Cell One. I slipped past the officers so I could step into the cell. I did not know what I would find, of course. I wish I had. I wish that trains that are going to become derailed were painted with warnings, or that black dots would appear on the faces of people who were soon to die. I wish the covers of books that I would not enjoy were printed with suggestions to read something else, although the names of certain authors are often warning enough. I wish I always knew when something dreadful was going to happen, because then I would not step into rooms where dreadful things could surprise me.

The train screeched to a jolty, awkward halt just as I entered the cell. The jolt almost threw me against the wall, but there was something else surprising, too. A smell. Metal, I thought. It smells metallic. Cell One was not much different from an ordinary compartment, with two benches and two racks and a table and, out the window, the dark scenery holding its breath. But there was something else, too. Anything with enough iron in it, I told myself, can smell metallic. Broccoli, for instance. Mackerel. Blood.

Death was in the room with me, like a bad guest. Dashiell Qwerty lay on the floor, amid the shiny fragments of a broken window. The checkered handkerchief he always carried was next to him, fluttering in the cold wind. His hand was clutched to his throat, where I could see blood spreading in a terrible stain. The librarian's face had already turned stark white, like the blank pages sometimes found in the back of a book. He did not move, of course. He would never read or move again. Dashiell Qwerty was dead, and standing over his body, trembling in a gray uniform, was the tall, wild-haired figure of S. Theodora Markson.

We invited villainy aboard, I thought. And now its terrible mess was everywhere I looked.

CHAPTER FIVE

This is my story, Officers. I boarded *The Thistle of the Valley* to take a trip with my friend Moxie Mallahan. I seem to have lost my ticket. I was unaware that either my associate S. Theodora Markson or the librarian Dashiell Qwerty was aboard the train. My friend and I were talking of this and that when we heard a commotion on the other side of the wall. The source of the commotion turned out to be Mr. Qwerty being murdered in his cell. Yes, I noticed that the window was broken. Yes, I noticed that Ms. Markson was in the cell standing over him. I do not know why she was there. I do not know why she was dressed as a train conductor. I do not know anything else that might help with the case. I do not know anything at all. Thank you. You're welcome.

The Officers Mitchum took down all this story with a pencil and a lot of frowning and nodding. I felt sick about the whole thing. We were in the corridor of the prison car, with the door to Cell One still hanging open like an arm bent the wrong way, and Cell Two locked up tight. At the very back of the car was a small dull door marked OFFICERS' LOUNGE in irritating letters, and out the dirty windows the landscape was still halted. The rocky bottom of the drained sea wasn't any help to me, and neither were the Mitchums.

"I don't like it," Harvey said, when I was done.

"I don't like it either," I said quietly. "The death of a librarian is a terrible thing."

"It's not just a terrible thing," Mimi said. "It's a crime."

Harvey frowned at her. "Mimi, a crime *is* a terrible thing."

"Not always. Jaywalking is a crime, but there's nothing so terrible about it."

"Jaywalking?"

"Jaywalking is walking across the street when you're not supposed to."

"I know what jaywalking is, Mimi. But only a dumbbell would bring up jaywalking in the middle of a murder investigation."

"Only a ding-a-ling would call me a dumbbell!"

Now I looked at them. The Officers Mitchum were not good at enforcing the law, but they were very good at arguing with one another. Normally I had no patience for it. With a librarian murdered I had less than no patience for it.

"Can we *please*," I said, "continue with the investigation?"

Harvey Mitchum wanted to give me a stern look, but couldn't quite look me in the eye. "There's nothing to investigate, lad."

"Harvey's right, for once in his life," said Mimi, who was also looking someplace else. "It's still too early to make assumptions, but it seems your chaperone will go to jail for a very long time."

In silence the Mitchums and I looked over at the only other person in the corridor. Theodora's head was down and her strange, lengthy hair hung over her face so I couldn't see it. My chaperone had been this way since the murder had been discovered. She had no more to say than Qwerty did. She just sat there, like a sulking child, while the bickering officers rushed to judgment, a phrase which here means "thought of her as a murderer." I didn't know what to think myself.

"You should at least talk to Moxie," I said. "She was with me in the next compartment."

"That girl won't be any help," Harvey scoffed. "You said yourself she couldn't have heard anything, so she's not a real witness."

"Well, then we'd better find some real witnesses," I said. *"The Thistle of the Valley* is full of passengers. Surely somebody knows something about Qwerty's murder. We'll canvass the neighborhood."

"Canvass the neighborhood" is a phrase which means "ask questions of everyone nearby," and it is a common practice among law enforcement officials, but the Mitchums frowned like they'd never heard of such a thing.

"This is a train, not a neighborhood," Mimi said, "and our uniforms are one hundred percent polyester."

"Good point, Mimi," Harvey said. "We don't need to be wasting our time with canvas."

"Well, I'm going to knock on a few doors," I said, "and see what I can find."

The knock came right then, at the sliding doors, and over the sound of the knock was another sound. I recognized the sound and I knew who was making it and I didn't like either of them. Mimi reached over my head and opened the doors for her son. Stew Mitchum had the ability to make the piercing noise of a police siren and was taking loud advantage of this ability now. He cut the siren when he met my gaze, and then just stood for a moment rocking back and forth on his heels and hating me with his eyes. His hair was a mess and his smile was nasty. Last I'd checked, Stew Mitchum had joined up with the Inhumane Society at Wade Academy, and I wondered if Stew had boarded the train just now, when it stopped at Offshore Island, or if he had been with his parents all along.

"Lollipop Licket," he said. "Who let you in here?"

"Stew Mitchum," I said. "Shouldn't you be in school?"

"That's an old question," Stew said. "If I were you, I wouldn't worry about my education. I'd worry about your chaperone. She's trapped, like a spider caught in a web."

"Spiders make webs," I said. "They don't get caught in them."

"I meant a fly," Stew growled.

"How in the world could a spider get caught in a fly?"

"Make all the jokes you want, Snicket. The librarian got dead, and we're going to make sure your old lady pays for her crime."

"She's not my old lady," I said, "and she's no murderer."

"Then why was she standing over Qwerty's body?" Harvey demanded, and I saw Theodora shudder beneath her conductor's jacket. This would have been a good time for Theodora to speak, instead of shudder. It would have been a good time for my chaperone to clear her name. It would have been a good time for truth, and for justice. Instead she just shuddered, so it fell to me to do the things it was a good time to do.

"We need to investigate further," I said.

Mimi looked at me, and I saw something in her eyes I could not quite define, like a word you've heard a myriad of times that you still don't quite know. It was not the usual look of bickery annoyance I saw from the Officers Mitchum. It was something shaky, or perhaps nervous. "I guess it's nice you want to help Theodora," she said. "You're fond of her, so you can't believe she's a criminal."

"I'll believe she's a criminal if the facts say she is," I said. "Right now we don't have the facts."

"We don't need the facts when we have the murderer," Stew snarled, and pointed a thick, sweaty finger at my chaperone. "In a few minutes this train will be back on its way to the city, where the authorities are waiting. Theodora will be sent to prison for murder, and that's that."

"That's not that," I said. "That's not even half of that. The authorities will want proof that the right person has been arrested. An investigation will provide that proof."

Harvey Mitchum gave his family a nervous glance, and then looked at me. "Investigate if you want to," he said, "but we're keeping Theodora with us until we sort things out."

"Things will be sorted out soon enough," I said, firmly and incorrectly.

"They're already sorted," Stew growled. "They're as sorted as dirty laundry."

"The authorities will want more than your grubby clothing," I said. "I'm canvassing this train and I'll find the truth."

"The truth," Stew muttered, and snorted. One of the truths of the world is that the world often snorts at the truth. It is an ugly sound, even uglier than Stew Mitchum imitating a siren, but still I was not relieved when the siren sound began again and the three Mitchums escorted Theodora to the back of the prisoners' car, through the door marked OFFICERS' LOUNGE, leaving me alone in the corridor.

First I went to the door of Cell Two. It was locked, of course. It's not a cell if the door isn't locked. I listened, but without a bottle to help me I only heard my own heartbeat and nothing else, so I went through the open door of Cell One and returned to the scene of the crime. The night air rustled at my jacket as I stepped carefully across the broken glass on the floor. Dear Kit, I am standing in a cell and looking at Dashiell Qwerty, covered in a sheet. I hope your evening is going better than mine.

Outside the window the dark landscape lay quiet and still, and I remembered that the train had stopped so that another passenger might come aboard and be caught, as Moxie had predicted, like a rat in a trap. I could not help but think that a rat was already on board. Certainly I smelled a rat in the way the investigation of Qwerty's death was proceeding. Get moving, Snicket, I told myself. Canvass the train. You've seen a librarian somebody wanted dead, in a room covered in broken glass. That's all you need.

I left the cell. The car was clear. I stepped back through the sliding doors and stood for a moment looking out the window of the train. Offshore Island had no proper train station, just a wide wooden platform from better days, when students would take *The Thistle of the Valley* to get a top-drawer education at Wade Academy. Now the platform looked cracked and done, with one dim light on a bent pole showing me what was there. What was there was nothing. There was no sign of any passenger, villainous or otherwise.

I walked past the door to Moxie's compartment, where she was still lying low, and rapped my knuckles on the neighboring door. There was a scuffle and a metallic *clang!* as if someone had dropped a soup pot.

"Who's there?" came a voice. The sound was muffled, and slightly buzzy, a sound I recognized from my apprenticeship. The citizens of Stain'd-by-the-Sea occasionally wore strange silver masks, with small slits for eyes and a metal filter where the mouth should have been. Some said the masks were absolutely necessary for medical reasons, and others said they were merely superstition. I had my own ideas. People usually donned these masks when a bell rang from the tower of Wade Academy, but I hadn't heard that signal. Perhaps it had been drowned out by the noises of the train.

"I asked who's there?" the voice repeated, and this time I thought I might recognize it, although it was difficult to tell, through a mask and a wooden door.

"Kenneth," I replied, thinking quickly.

There was a short pause.

"Kenneth who?"

"Kenneth Grahame."

The Scottish author Kenneth Grahame and the title of his most famous and second-best book, *The Wind in the Willows*, had come to serve as a code between my associates and me. During our investigation of Wade Academy, we had used the name of the author, Kenneth Grahame, to identify who was with us and who was against us. The code worked, and the door opened. My associate was removing a mask and putting on an astonished expression as I stepped into the compartment.

"Lemony Snicket," he said. "What are you doing here?"

"Kellar Haines," I said. "I have the same question."

He closed the door behind me, and looked around the compartment as if a villain were hiding in the luggage rack. He was wearing a long, loose raincoat, like one you might borrow from your uncle or bodyguard, and his hair as usual was tilted into a spike. He put the mask down on a bench, and I wondered why he had been in disguise when I'd knocked. "I don't think I should tell you," he said. "You're the one who said we should be keeping quiet and working against Hangfire in solitude."

"Well, you're not in solitude," I said. "Moxie Mallahan is on board *The Thistle of the Valley*. She's the reason for this unscheduled stop."

Kellar fiddled nervously with his spiky hair. "Moxie's here?"

"She's in the compartment next door."

"What is she doing?"

"You'd better ask her yourself, Haines. I'm on an investigation of my own."

His eyes searched mine, which I hoped looked less nervous. He put his hands deep in the pockets of his raincoat, like an anxious puppeteer. "Something's happened, hasn't it, Snicket?"

"Did you hear or see anything suspicious," I asked, "right before the train came to a stop?"

Kellar shook his head slowly. "I've been lying low since I got on board," he said. "I've hardly heard or seen a thing besides the noise of the train and the landscape outside."

"I was afraid of that."

"You look afraid of more than that, Snicket. Something bad happened. I can tell by your face."

"My mouth will tell you the rest of it, Haines, but I've got to move quickly. You should, too. Hurry up and go to Moxie."

"I'm hurryupping," he said, using a word I'd never heard until I'd met Kellar. He and his unusual raincoat were both out the door in seconds, so I was alone in the compartment when a long, shrill sound startled its way through the night. It was the sound that had interrupted my early bedtime and begun the last chapter of my

days in Stain'd-by-the-Sea. It was a train whistle, and with great grinding and complaining
The Thistle of the Valley began to move again. I
stepped out into the corridor and watched the
platform roll out of view. Offshore Island was
the last chance, I thought, before *The Thistle
of the Valley* took us all to the city. It was another
thing I was wrong about. But the platform was
still empty. Has anyone come aboard, I wondered, or was the train stopping another trick of
Hangfire's?

I was getting curious. I'd almost forgotten.
I'd remembered to be sad, at the death of a noble
librarian, and I'd remembered to be angry, at
the way the Officers Mitchum were handling the
case. I'd even remembered to be annoyed, when
Stew had imitated a siren, and when Gifford and
Ghede had clogged up the corridor. But you cannot solve a mystery simply by being sad, angry,
and annoyed. You need to get curious. You need
to get curious the way you get curious when

you find a piece of something—a coiled metal spring, a scrap of torn paper, a smooth white bone—and you want to know the rest of it. My hand crinkled the paper train in my pocket, and the paper train crinkled back. What is it? I thought. What is the rest? Ornette's message was part of a mystery. Theodora stealing a uniform was part of the mystery, and it was part of the mystery that she boarded the train. Sally Murphy was part of the mystery, back at Stain'd Station with the strange porter. Sharon Haines was part of the mystery, suddenly appearing in the station, and Kellar Haines was part of it, suddenly appearing on board, and even Moxie Mallahan was part of it, with the cardboard Bombinating Beast that would or would not lure Hangfire to his defeat. Were Gifford and Ghede part of the mystery too? Were the Officers Mitchum? And what about all the other passengers, Snicket, all the doors you need to knock on to find the truth? It was a great number of questions, scattered around my mind like books that had fallen to the floor and needed to be shelved and cataloged. But the librarian is dead, Snicket. That's the saddest and most terrifying part of the mystery, the part as dark as the landscape outside the windows. Dashiell Qwerty had the information to stop Hangfire. He said so himself, right before he was murdered. He'd learned the truth, and now you're looking for the truth yourself. But the truth is like a doorknob. You can stumble around in the dark, and when you finally grasp it, you may end up someplace terrifying.

I headed down the corridor to do my job. You got curious, I told myself, as I began to canvass the train. You got curious, but just make sure that you don't get dead.

CHAPTER SIX

The Thistle of the Valley clattered through the night. Criminals were afoot and so was I, stepping back into the corridor and pushing open the sliding doors that led to the next passenger car. I had to knock loudly on the compartment door so I could be heard over the sounds of the train, and I had to lean in to hear the sounds that came from behind the door. There was some gasping and some rustling and a big *shh* that came too late.

I knocked again. This time the silence was performed a little better.

"I know you're in there," I said, and opened the door. What I'd said was true, although I did not know who the "you" was until I stepped into the compartment and took a look. It was a boy, sitting on the bench with a bright blue jacket wadded up next to him. At least, he appeared to be a boy older than I was. He was not much taller than I was but had a small patch of beard on his chin. My chin hadn't developed the ability to grow a beard, but when it did, I thought, I wouldn't grow a beard like that. It was a small, dark square, more like a business card than a beard, and it hung from his face as if it had been hurriedly taped there. All in all it was a startling sight, and the person standing next to the boy was startling too, although she shouldn't have been. So many unexpected appearances, I thought. It's like a haunted house or a surprise party, two things I've never enjoyed.

112

"You again," said Sally Murphy.

"Me again," I said back.

"I thought we left you behind at Stain'd Station," the actress said.

"No such luck," I said. "I'm conducting an investigation. Did you hear or see anything suspicious right before the train came to a stop?"

Sally Murphy was already shaking her head. "Neither of us did," she said, without even consulting her companion. "Why do you ask?"

"I'm sorry to say that a crime has been committed on board this train."

"A crime?" Sally Murphy repeated, as if the word were unfamiliar to her, rather than a recent hobby of hers. "Is that why the train came to a stop before?"

"No," I said, and the actress and the boy exchanged nervous glances. "A murder was committed, just before *The Thistle of the Valley* made its unscheduled stop."

Neither passenger replied or even looked

at me. They were still looking at each other. A mention of murder hadn't made them as nervous as the train's unscheduled stop.

"I'm hoping to find a witness," I said, "or anyone who can provide useful information."

Sally Murphy blinked and turned to me. "We didn't witness anything," she said quickly, "and we're certainly not useful. We've been hiding in this compartment since the train left Stain'd Station. *Ow!*"

The actress rubbed her arm and looked at the other passenger. It looked like she'd been given a hard poke. "Not *hiding*," she said quickly. "*Sitting*, I meant to say. Yes, we've just been sitting here."

Sally Murphy sat down and crossed her arms, which I noticed were trembling. The person next to her seemed to be trembling, too—trembling so hard that the beard looked in danger of falling off his face and fluttering down to the wooden bench, where the blue jacket lay crumpled. "I suppose this is your nephew or something," I said to the actress.

"I don't have a nephew," Sally Murphy said, and then jumped a little. "*Ow!* I mean, of course I have a nephew. He's a real live nephew and he's sitting right there."

"So I see," I said. "He's sitting next to a bright blue jacket with a thistle in the lapel, just like porters wear at Stain'd Station."

"I don't think that's any of your business," the actress said.

"Well, I happen to think it is," I said. "I've made a number of things my business. The theft of a statue, for instance. A great number of children going missing, for instance, including a young woman whose brother is frantic to find her. And now the murder of a librarian is my business, so I'm canvassing the train, looking for anything suspicious, which is why I notice things left out on compartment benches."

115

Sally Murphy leaned back and then forward, like it was her first dance lesson. "I—" she said.

"Don't worry if your performance doesn't fool me," I said. "I'm not a drama critic. But some people think this train stopped to let on another passenger who might be even more interested in your performance than I am."

The actress blinked at me.

"His name is Hangfire," I said, and her eyes widened with fear. I remembered her screams in the basement of the Sallis mansion as it filled up with water from an underground well. She was terrified then, and the incident is described in an earlier report of mine, in case you feel like being terrified yourself. "You said at the station that you could never escape from Hangfire," I reminded her now, "but tonight we may have an opportunity to stop his treachery."

"If Hangfire is aboard this train," Sally Murphy said, "there'll be no stopping him."

"If Hangfire's aboard," I said, "he'll see right

through you. Porters' uniforms don't lie around on trains unless a retired grocer helps someone's nephew with a disguise."

"No one's wearing a disguise," Sally Murphy said quickly.

"Then get rid of that," I said, pointing to the jacket, "and hurry up about it."

"I'm hurryupping," muttered the nephew, and he began to fold up the uniform while Sally Murphy gave me a trembly frown.

"And you hurry up out of here, Snicket," she said. "You have no idea what is going on."

I looked at the actress, and then at her mysterious companion, and then left the compartment without so much as a "good-bye" or a "so long" or a "This mystery continues to confound me." She was right. I had no idea what was going on. Wherever I turned, there were surprising people and mysterious schemes afoot, and I was no closer to finding Qwerty's murderer. I looked out the window at the dark and racing scenery and I thought of the city, where the train would eventually arrive. I hadn't seen the city since my apprenticeship began, and for a moment I felt so homesick I had to stop and lean my head against the glass. Dear Kit, I thought. And then I said it out loud.

"I wish you were here."

My voice was quiet. Kit didn't answer. Nobody did. I let myself rest against the window for ten more seconds, and when twenty seconds were up I stood and walked to the next compartment door. Continue your canvass, Snicket, I thought to myself. See what there is to see.

I knocked on the door while opening it, the way parents do to children, which leads to a lot of shrieking about privacy. The occupants of the compartment said nothing about privacy. There were three of them, all strangers and all sitting on one of the benches, quiet as cans of soup. One was a man with a very round, very bald head, and very round, very thick glasses around his eyes.

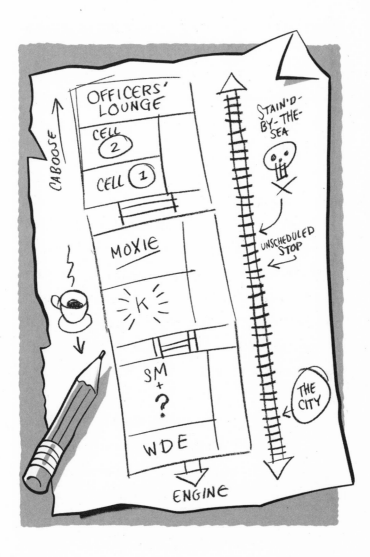

Next to him was a heavily sweatered woman, either old enough to be the man's mother or young enough to be his wife but hadn't gotten enough sleep lately, and then a very old man with a gray beard that grew out in two different directions, like a split in a river. On the small table near the window were three thick books. None of them had the same title or the same author, but they all had the same thing on the spine. Next to the books were a few pencils and scraps of paper, held together with rubber bands, and more pencils and scraps of paper tucked here and there in more books stacked up in the racks above their heads. I knew what the books meant, and the pencils and the scraps of paper. Anyone from my organization would have known.

"Good evening," I said, and the wind whistled through the compartment's window, which was open just a tiny bit. It ruffled the scraps of paper, but no one made a move to close it. "I'm Lemony Snicket."

"Walleye," the bald man said.

"Pocket," said the woman.

"I'm Eratosthenes," said the man with the unusual beard, the only one who met my eyes. His own eyes looked like they were asking me something, but I did not know what it was.

"I'm sorry to disturb you," I said, "but I'm in the middle of an important investigation. Did any of you hear or see anything suspicious, right before the train came to a stop?"

The wind ruffled the papers again. Everyone looked at the papers, and then at the window, and then at me.

"I'm afraid a murder has been committed," I said, and the wind blew again, a bit harder. A few scraps fluttered down to the carpet. The three strangers watched them flutter.

"I'm on the lookout for anything suspicious," I said, "like for instance, three people keeping very quiet and still when a murder has been announced, not even moving to close the window."

121

Eratosthenes gave a sort of growl, and stood up. The two ends of his beard pointed in two different directions, but his finger, bony and pale, pointed at me. "Shut the window yourself, if you want it shut," he said. "Open it if you want it open. Climb out of it or climb back in. We'll say anything you want us to say. Just leave us alone."

"We're peaceful people," said Pocket, "and we want no part of this."

"Point your dart gun at someone else," Wall-eye said.

"Dart gun?" I said, but the three passengers might not have heard me over the sound of a siren in the corridor. The wooden door opened, and a number of people walked into the compartment. First came the Officers Mitchum, Harvey leading the way and Mimi telling him that she should be leading the way. Then came Theodora, still looking pale and still looking at the ground, and then came Theodora's hair, which took longer to enter the room than she did. Bringing up the rear, which was where he belonged, was Stew Mitchum, whose mouth stopped imitating a siren and started smirking as soon as he saw me.

"I'm glad you're here," he said. "We've found the real witnesses you were blabbering about. These three people witnessed Dashiell Qwerty's murder. Thanks to them, your precious Theodora will be locked up for good."

"My chaperone is not a murderer," I said, but Theodora didn't even raise her head. Stew smiled the sort of smile that fools many adults but never a single child, and he walked over to the bench.

"Tell me," he said to the passengers, "did you hear or see anything suspicious, right before the train came to a stop?"

The three strangers looked at one another, like they were in line to walk the plank. Stew kept up his grin. Some people are trouble from the moment you meet them, and Stew Mitchum was one of those people. But he was also the sort of person who got worse, like a small cut on your hand that you don't bother to take care of. First it hurts, and then it hurts worse, and before you know it people faint dead away at the sight of the gruesome and bloody mess you have on your hands.

"Well?" Harvey demanded. "Are you a witness to this crime?"

Walleye cleared his throat and looked at his two companions. "Yes," he said, in a "yes" that sounded very much like a "no."

"What's your name?"

"Walleye," said Walleye.

"Occupation?"

"Harvey, what does it matter what he does for a living?" Mimi asked her husband with a sigh, and then turned to Walleye. "Tell us what you heard."

The bald man sighed, like there was medicine

he had to take. "I heard two people fighting in Cell One," he said.

"You couldn't have heard that," I said. "Your compartment is nowhere near the prison car. Passengers much closer to the crime said they didn't hear a thing."

The woman coughed, a rough sound over the clattering of the train. "My name is Pocket," she said, like she was reading it off an eye chart. "My occupation is—"

"Never mind that," Harvey interrupted. "What did you see?"

"I saw S. Theodora Markson shoot Dashiell Qwerty with a poison dart."

"You did no such thing," I said.

The old man looked the most scared of all. "Eratosthenes is my name," he said, "and my occupation is the same as the others. I saw that stranger over there, S. Theodora Markson, throw the weapon out the window of the train when she was done, and I heard the glass shatter on the floor."

"If she's a total stranger," I said, "how do you know her name?"

"I'm asking the questions here," Harvey Mitchum barked, "and I have no further questions for this witness. The case is closed. I'll write up my report and deliver Theodora to the authorities when the train reaches the city."

There's a kind of astonishment you can taste in your throat, a burning angry flavor that made me spit out my words. "This is absurd," I said, and the Mitchums turned to me in anxious unison, a phrase which here means that they did it at the same time and with the same sickly look. "Theodora is being railroaded."

"Well," Mimi said, "she is on a train."

"'Railroaded' is a word which here means 'framed for a crime,'" I said, and though it was the right definition it was the wrong thing to say. I looked at Theodora. Her head was still down

126

and her hair was still in her face, and she had twisted her hands together like she was already in handcuffs.

"You saw her yourself, lad," Harvey said, his voice trembling slightly, "standing in the cell, next to Qwerty's body. I hate to tell you this, but your chaperone is a murderer. We're locking her up now and she'll go to trial in the city."

"You can't lock her up in Qwerty's cell," Mimi said. "She could escape through the broken window."

"I know that, Mimi," Harvey said sharply. "You think I don't know that? I'm putting Theodora in Cell Two with the other prisoner."

"A cell is not a sandwich, Harvey. You can't ask people to share it."

"Qwerty shared his."

I thought of all the murmuring voices I had heard before the shattering of glass. "With whom?" I asked.

Harvey and Mimi exchanged a quick, guilty

127

look. "That's the wrong question," Mimi said to me. "In fact, there are no more questions. You said the authorities would want proof, and now you have it. Three witnesses say Theodora is the murderer."

I walked closer and closer to the bickering officers until I stood face to face with them, or face to badge, as they were both taller than I was. The badges had lost most of their shine and looked like they were quite tired of being pinned to the people they were pinned to. I stared at them for a second and then looked the Officers Mitchum right in their eyes. Between the two of them, and their four eyes, I saw not one speck of courage. Get scared later, is what I wanted to tell them, but they were scared now. "Why are you doing this?" I asked them, instead.

The two Mitchums shared a look again. "You know why," Harvey murmured, just barely.

"We're the law," Mimi told me quietly, as if she did not believe a word of it, "from the outskirts of town in the hinterlands to the boundary of the Clusterous Forest. And we're telling you that Theodora is guilty."

She put one hand on my chaperone's shoulder, and Harvey put his hand on the other. "This is wrong," I said, but I do not know if the Mitchums even heard me, because the compartment rang with a loud, shaky noise. For a moment I thought the train had been derailed, but I turned and realized Stew had pounded his fist on the wall. He shot a dark look every which way, finally settling on the Mitchums as if he wanted to tear his parents limb from limb. Everyone wants to tear their parents limb from limb sometimes, but Stew looked like he might do something about it. His parents looked away, and the three witnesses looked at the ground. Theodora looked nowhere, just allowed herself to be led out of the compartment by the two officers, with their sneering son following. I turned to the three passengers on the bench. "Do you know what you've done?" I asked them. "Because of your testimony, an innocent woman has been framed for the death of a friend of mine."

The strangers said nothing.

"A terrible villain has been terrorizing a community, and because of your lies he's going to continue," I said. "There's treachery afoot, and thanks to you, it's going to stay afoot a little bit longer." The strangers added nothing to the nothing they had already said.

"Would it make a difference," I asked them, "if I told you that the murder victim was a librarian—just like you?"

The three strangers looked like they'd been punched in the stomach, and then like they wanted to punch back. "How did you know?" Walleye sputtered.

"Lots of library books," I said, "pencils and scrap paper, shabby but stylish clothing. It's not much of a mystery, if one has worked with librarians all one's life. Giacomo Casanova was a noble librarian. So was Marcel Duchamp, and that goes double for Beverly Cleary. But you three are disgraces to the profession, and you know it."

"Now see here, young man—" Eratosthenes started.

"I'm trying to see here," I said. "I'm trying to see the solution to this mystery, but I don't know where to look. Normally in a situation like this I'd ask a librarian for help. But the best librarian in these parts is dead, and you three are too busy being ashamed of yourselves to even pick up the books you brought with you." I slammed out of the compartment as scornfully as I could, although not as scornfully as I wanted. I stood in the corridor feeling like an angry pebble. It didn't matter where I rolled off to. The mystery and treachery of the world continued, and a pebble like me could get angry over anything it liked and it wouldn't do any good. Librarians not reading, I thought to myself. Sometimes I don't know why I bother.

I stood stewing about it for a minute, until I heard the sound of the sliding doors opening and some heavy, unpleasant footsteps. You haven't heard the footsteps of a bully until you've heard them coming for you.

"You ought to change your name to Necktie," Stew Mitchum said. "You're always hanging around."

"Your parents aren't going to solve this crime," I said, "so why shouldn't I keep investigating?"

"Because I said so," Stew said.

" 'Because I said so' is the worst reason on Earth," I said, and I turned to face him. He looked steadily at me and then moved all ten of his fingers, like he was making sure he had two fists if he needed them.

"Listen up, Lemonade," he said, using an insulting nickname I was tired of when I was four. "This is one of those violent threats you've read about. You're going to stop your investigation and retire to your compartment to play with your little pals. I'm going to give you to the count of Get Out of Here Right Now."

"That's not a number."

"You want a number?" Stew showed me what his fist looked like. "I'll do a number on you."

"I'm not a stroller," I said. "You can't push me around. I'm going to find out the truth about Dashiell Qwerty's murder."

"We'll see what you find out," Stew said. "You'll find out what it feels like to be thrown from a speeding train to the rocky bottom of a drained sea. Except you won't really find out, because you'll be dead. Get it? What I mean is, it'll kill you when I throw you from this train, so you'll be in no state to find out what it feels like. Get it? Due to your death by falling from a train."

"I get it, I get it," I said. Violent threats are less effective when they need serious editing.

Stew offered me a triumphant smirk, the way you'd offer someone a poisoned muffin. I didn't want it. Then he turned and stomped off, quickly and carelessly, which is probably why he didn't notice the small object I saw on the floor. I noticed it, though. I was the person who was supposed to notice it. With a quick glance at Stew's departing figure, I leaned down to pluck it off the carpet, like it was a delicate creature I was trying to capture and study, and slipped it into my pocket. My mind felt like soil must feel when a tiny sprout starts pushing its way through. Don't look at it here, I told myself. It's not safe here. This train is loaded with treachery and deceit, and rattling with deception and murder. Moxie doesn't even know, I realized, as I retraced my steps. You're going to have to tell her that Dashiell Qwerty is dead, and that S. Theodora has been railroaded. You're going to have to bring her all the bad news. I trudged my way back to Moxie's compartment and opened the door with a heavy heart and a weary head. But when I stepped inside, my heart and head only got heavier and wearier. Moxie Mallahan and Kellar Haines were both there, huddled over Moxie's typewriter, and they both looked up at me as I entered. *The Thistle of the Valley* hummed underneath my feet like an escalator or an earthquake, a dark buzzing sound. Through the window I could see the dim silhouette of the Clusterous Forest as we approached, the great mass of seaweed that had somehow survived the draining of the sea and now lived to shiver in the breeze. But on the table beneath the window was a more troubling sight. Two black statues, with sharp teeth and empty eyes, sat staring at me with identical malevolence. "Malevolence" is a word for the sort of evil that is dark and shiny, as dark and shiny as the Bombinating Beast.

"Lemony Snicket," Moxie said, "I'm afraid we have some bad news."

CHAPTER SEVEN

"What's the news?" I asked, and sat down on one of the compartment's wooden benches. I was talking to my associates, but I was still looking at the two Bombinating Beasts on the table. I stared and stared, unsteady from the rattling train and from the eerie sight. What are you, I asked them silently. What do you want with me? Since I'd arrived in Stain'd-by-the-Sea, the questions about a mysterious item had hovered in my mind like stars, bright and cold and impossible to get ahold of. Now there were two of them, right in front of me, but I felt no closer to understanding what was really going on.

"We've stumbled into quicksand," Moxie said with a sigh. "Remember when we all agreed to work quietly, so Hangfire wouldn't learn of our plot to defeat him? Well, Haines and I both worked quietly on the same scheme."

Kellar kicked at the bad carpet. "I asked Ornette if she could make a copy of the Bombinating Beast," he said, "and then I got a message to Hangfire arranging to trade the statue for the safe return of my sister."

"The jig is up," Moxie said glumly. "Hangfire received both of our messages, so he knew we were tricking him."

"But the train made its unscheduled stop," Kellar said.

"That was to trick *us*," Moxie replied. "There's no way he came aboard."

"Do you think so, Snicket?" Kellar asked. "Do you think the jig is really up?"

I thought so and I told him so. He took it as well as he could, a phrase which here means he looked defeated and sad. Moxie put her hand on his shoulder.

"I'm sorry, Haines," she said.

Kellar patted her hand. "It's not your fault," he said, "but I thought for a moment we could defeat Hangfire."

"If he'd come aboard, he'd be caught like a rat in a trap," Moxie said.

Kellar looked out the window of the train. It was not too dark to see the seaweed of the Clusterous Forest, billowing like smoke and coming closer and closer as the train rattled along. "If he'd come aboard," he said quietly, "I might have rescued my sister."

"Ornette must have realized what was going on," I said, and took the folded train out of my pocket. "She knew there'd be trouble on *The Thistle of the Valley.*"

"I caught a glimpse of you at Stain'd Station, Snicket," Kellar said, "but just when I was about to approach you, I was spotted."

Moxie put a fresh piece of paper in her typewriter, and began typing this up. "Who spotted you?" she asked.

"My mother," Kellar said darkly. "I guess a mother can't miss her own child in a crowd."

That made me think of something, but it was Moxie who asked the question. "What was she doing at the station?"

"Trying to stop me from coming aboard," Kellar said grimly. "I can't believe she's still working with the Inhumane Society."

"Mothers do all sorts of things nobody can believe," I said. "We're in the middle of a quagmire, a word which here means 'heap of trouble.'"

Moxie gave me a small smile. "Why do you always say that—*which here means?*"

"I'll probably outgrow it," I said.

Her smile stopped. "What is it, Snicket? Where have you been all this time? What happened when you were listening to the prisoners' car?"

"Something's happened," Kellar said. "I knew it the minute you found me on board. What is it?"

What it was then was a knock on the door, and Moxie looked frantically at the two statues on the table. I went to the door and reached for the latch, while Kellar stood in front of the table with his arms out wide to block the view as best he could, as if the Bombinating Beasts were a birthday present no one had bothered to wrap yet.

"Who's there?" I asked.

"Kenneth Grahame," came the reply, and of course when I opened the door it was not one Scottish author but one chemist and one cook who were sweethearts of each other's and associates of mine. My spirits rose a little. With Jake

Hix and Cleo Knight aboard, we had a full team of volunteers, honest and brave and with a fierce enthusiasm for literature. It might not be enough to defeat the evil aboard *The Thistle of the Valley*, I thought, but it is better to fail among friends.

"We came as soon as we got the message," Jake said, and took out a folded paper train identical to mine. "Cleo drove the Dilemma at top speed."

The Dilemma was an automobile, powerfully handsome and handsomely powerful, that had gotten us out of a few troublesome situations and was very fun to ride around in when there were no troublesome situations to be found. "I thought I saw your headlights out the window," I said.

Cleo nodded. "I thought we were going to have to pull some crazy stunt to get on board *The Thistle of the Valley*. I wanted to leap onto the train and use the railings to climb aboard, but Jake said it was too dangerous."

"Those railings would never hold," Jake said.

"Not for long, anyway," I agreed, with a still-sore knee.

"But then the train stopped at Offshore Island," Cleo said, "and we managed to sneak aboard. We practically had to canvass the train to find you. What's the plan? What's with those statues? How are we going to defeat Hangfire? How did you get him to come aboard?"

"Hangfire's not here," Kellar said. "He saw through our scheme like it was a fishbowl. Moxie and I both tried to lure him onto *The Thistle of the Valley*, but it's no dice."

"No dice" is an expression which means "That is not going to happen," but Jake shook his head as if there were plenty of dice after all. "Don't be so sure," he said. "Cleo and I saw a masked figure climb aboard, just as the train pulled to a stop."

"Hangfire?" Moxie said.

"Who else could it be?" Jake asked.

"Stew Mitchum opened the door for him," Cleo said, her mouth curled down the way any of our mouths did when we talked about Stew, "in the very back of the very last car."

"The Officers' Lounge," I remembered, "in the very back of the prisoners' car."

"The car where Qwerty was locked up," Moxie said thoughtfully.

"And Ellington Feint," I said.

"Never mind Ellington Feint," Moxie said with a frown.

"If Hangfire's here," Kellar said hopefully, "maybe our messages fooled him after all."

I shook my head. "Hangfire knew it was a trick," I said, "but he came aboard anyway. He's the one who's set a trap, and all of us are the rats in it."

"Don't call us rats, Snicket," Jake said. "Hangfire boarded alone. There are more of us than there are of him. Whatever treachery he's planning, we can stop it before it starts."

"It started already," I said. "It started before *The Thistle of the Valley* left Stain'd-by-the-Sea. It started before my early bedtime. It started before I read a single book Dashiell Qwerty recommended."

This was the sort of thing that Moxie would normally type up, but she wasn't even looking at her typewriter. She was looking at me.

"What is it, Snicket?" she said.

"Sit down," Cleo said to me gently. "You're looking pale."

She helped me onto a bench, and Moxie reached over to put a hand on my cheek. It was something my sister used to do to me, when I was very young, to show me she was listening. Dear Kit, I thought. I very much hate to deliver bad news.

"Snicket?" Moxie asked. "What happened?"

"I have some bad news" is what managed to come out of my mouth, as shaky as the train.

Moxie kept one hand on me, but she put the

other on the typewriter. "I knew it," she said. "What happened in the prison car?"

"Something awful," Kellar said. "I can tell."

"Tell us, Snicket," Moxie said, and I told them.

The Thistle of the Valley shook and clattered, but nobody else said anything. Bad news can hit you like a train. It will knock you over and leave you flat, but everybody else keeps rushing along.

"It's not true," Moxie said. "It can't be true."

I stayed where I was. There was no need to say it was true.

Jake rubbed at both his eyes with both his fists. "I wouldn't know who Eleanor Estes was if it weren't for Qwerty," he said. "I wouldn't know Lowry. I wouldn't know Snyder. Dashiell Qwerty was a great, great librarian."

"One of the greatest," I agreed.

Cleo shivered. "And they really think Theodora killed him?"

"Well, they locked her in a cell," I said.

Moxie reached toward her typewriter, but I watched her fingers tremble on the keys. "A real journalist knows that a murder is a big story," she said. "She'd type up her notes and cry about it later."

"There's nothing wrong with mourning the death of a librarian," I said.

Moxie looked at me. "Then why aren't you crying, Snicket?"

"I planned on doing it later," I said, but I cried a little right then. Everyone joined me. There is no point in delaying crying. Sadness is like having a vicious alligator around. You can ignore it for only so long before it begins devouring things and you have to pay attention. I cried and then cried a little more and thought. Poor Qwerty, is what I thought. Poor sub-librarian. He keeps watch over Stain'd-by-the-Sea's library for ten years, and then it ends on a rattly train. Lemony Snicket comes into town, I thought, and everything gets worse for you, Qwerty. Snicket's a nice enough kid, but when you allow him into a library, you might as well flood the place and kill the brave and careful man who runs it. All of us cried in the rattling room, and the beasts watched over us and said nothing.

"How could she do it, Snicket?" Moxie said finally, wiping her eyes. "How could she kill him?"

"Take some notes," I told her, and then I told her about what I'd heard when I eavesdropped on Theodora and Qwerty. I told her about my canvassing of *The Thistle of the Valley*, and I told her about the three so-called witnesses who helped my chaperone get railroaded. Moxie was still shaky at first, but by the time I described the shattering of glass, the typewriter was going lickety-split.

"It sounds like Qwerty was in V.F.D., too," Jake said, "and we didn't even know it."

"I thought he might be," I said. "Most librarians are, of course."

148

Kellar scratched the spike in his hair. "Why didn't you ask him if he was one of us?"

"You don't ask if someone has integrity and pluck and has read a great many books in the hope of repairing the world," I said. "You just watch them, and figure it out for yourself."

"Why would Theodora," Cleo said, "kill someone who has integrity and pluck and has read a great many books in the hope of repairing the world?"

"She wouldn't."

"Are you sure, Snicket?" Kellar asked me. "Not so long ago, she wanted to leave town and abandon Stain'd-by-the-Sea to Hangfire's treachery."

"I have many complaints about my chaperone," I said, "but that doesn't make her a murderer."

"She's not a murderer," Jake said, with a disgusted wave of his hand, "just like Dashiell Qwerty was no arsonist. It couldn't have happened like those witnesses said."

"I know it didn't," I agreed. "I stood in that cell myself. It was full of broken glass. If Theodora had thrown the weapon out the window, like the witnesses told me, the glass would have fallen outside."

"But how do you explain Theodora stealing that uniform?" Cleo asked.

"She wanted to talk to a prisoner," I said. "Conductors are the only ones who would be allowed into the cells in the prison car. She argued with Qwerty, but he was killed by somebody else."

"I can't imagine Dashiell Qwerty having too many enemies," Jake said.

"Anyone who finds a crucial secret ends up with enemies," I said. "Qwerty had information that could stop Hangfire, and now he's dead."

"Do you think Hangfire snuck aboard this train and killed him?" Moxie asked.

I looked at the cardboard beasts and then at the dark, fast view out the window. "Hangfire doesn't do all of his treachery himself," I said. "He has plenty of people to help him."

"You're thinking of Ellington Feint again," Moxie said, with a severe frown.

"I'm thinking of everyone," I said. "Sally Murphy, Gifford and Ghede, Stew Mitchum—there are countless suspicious people on board *The Thistle of the Valley*, and those are just the ones we know about."

"Why not go to the Mitchums again," Cleo asked, "and tell them everything?"

"Because I don't know everything," I said. "Not yet. According to the law from the outskirts of town in the hinterlands to the boundary of the Clusterous Forest, the case is closed. But I can't seem to get the case open. Wherever I go on this train, there's a piece of a sinister plot, but I can't put the pieces in order."

"Dashiell Qwerty was murdered in his cell," Jake said. "That's the biggest piece."

"And there's Theodora, wrongly accused," Cleo said.

Moxie looked at her notes. "There are three librarians," she said, "dishonest and scared."

Kellar looked at the table. "There are two Bombinating Beasts, both decoys."

"There's Gifford and Ghede," I said, "disguised as conductors. And there's Sally Murphy, preparing for the role of a lifetime."

"And there are all those children at Wade Academy," Moxie said, with a shudder, "in the clutches of the Inhumane Society, stealing honeydews and preparing for goodness knows what."

"It's all a big question mark," Jake said, with a grim grin, and I gave him a fraught frown to match. Question marks made me think of Ellington Feint's curved eyebrows, and the smile she always gave me, that could have meant anything. It made me unsteady to think of all of it, and the train rattling made me feel unsteadier still.

"What are we going to do about it?" Moxie asked. "We have to try something. There's too much at stake. Like Theodora's freedom."

"Like Lizzie's life," Kellar said.

"Like our whole town's survival," Cleo said quietly. "Can we do it, Snicket? Can we really save Stain'd-by-the-Sea before it's gone completely?"

"Do we want it enough?" I asked. "Enough to do anything and everything?"

"V.F.D. represents the true human tradition," Moxie said, quoting a speech I had given to my associates at Wade Academy. "We represent the one permanent victory over cruelty and chaos."

"I don't know if we have everything necessary to be victorious over cruelty and chaos," I said.

She looked up from her typewriter and tilted her hat at me. "What is necessary?"

"Cruelty and chaos," I said, and stood up.

Moxie stopped typing. "Where are you going, Snicket?"

"To see Hangfire," I said.

Jake frowned. "Don't kid around."

"I'm not the kind of kid who kids," I told him. "Hangfire's at the middle of this mystery. It's my job to investigate it. I was wrong to canvass *The Thistle of the Valley* and look for suspects, when all along I knew this was his handiwork. I'm going to find him and talk to him."

"And what will you say?" Cleo asked.

"I think I'll start with 'Good evening.'"

Kellar shook his head. "You said yourself it's a trap, Snicket."

"I did," I said, "but I'm wrong all the time."

Moxie started to pack up her typewriter. "We're going with you."

"No," I said. "You stay here, all of you. It's time for you to stop working separately. Continue this investigation as best you can, so you can have a complete report in case."

"In case what?" Jake asked.

I looked out the window. The Clusterous

Forest was getting closer. "In case I don't come back," I said.

"You're crazy to go by yourself," Kellar said. "Hangfire has associates on this train. You still have bruises from some of them."

Cleo nodded. "How are you going to roam around this train without getting caught?" she asked, but then the question was answered by a noise out the window. It was the bell at Wade Academy, sounding the alarm, fainter than I'd ever heard it because of the distance the train had taken us. But it was loud enough to work. Moxie walked over to the other bench and lifted up the hinged seat. The silver masks were waiting there, like lifejackets aboard a sinking ship. She handed me one and gave me a sort of salute. A salute, if done right, is like a handshake, a hug, and some brave and noble words, all rolled into one silent gesture. I gave her one back that I hoped was as good.

"Kenneth Grahame," she told me.

"He's not the only noble author," I said. "There's Dahl."

"Sendak," Moxie said, and all my associates chimed in.

"Konigsburg."

"Brown."

"Gorey."

"Grimm," I said. It was a good way to leave. Outside the compartment I put the silver mask on my face and heard my own breathing turn sinister. The train shook in the dark, and I stood in the corridor and thought of the dark and shaky things surrounding me. I reached into my pocket and brought out the object I had retrieved from the floor. You should have told them about it, I thought. You said it was time to stop working separately. But if you had shown it to them, perhaps they never would have let you go. It was Ornette Lost's most impressive work yet. I kept looking at it. She had taken one of her business cards—if I looked carefully, I could still see the typed word "sculptor"—to make a round base, and then somehow attached a small square of black cardboard which was fashioned into a familiar shape. And then something I recognized but couldn't identify was attached on the top, a wafting of folded steam so delicate it fluttered with my breath. The whole sculpture looked so convincing that for a moment I thought it would shatter if it fell.

It was a tiny cup, the kind that holds coffee, steaming and perched on a saucer. You could be wrong, I reminded myself. You've been wrong about so much. But still, there's no reason to stop now. Keep going, no matter how wrong you are. Keep on the tracks, cross the bridges over the empty sea, clatter down to the edge of the Clusterous Forest. Get to the end of the mystery, Snicket. It's wrong for a young man to walk alone through a train moving alone through a valley of darkness, but it would be wrong to do anything else.

The Café Compartment looked for the most part like every other compartment. They'd removed one of the benches and put up a counter with a bowl of fruit that looked as tired as Moxie had said. The rack above the counter had sacks of coffee beans, and there was coffee bubbling away in a pot that smelled like last week's campfire. There was a small table with two little chairs, and in one of the chairs was a masked figure, staring out the window and holding a sad-looking apple. The figure made no move as I came in, and said nothing as I walked to the counter and looked things over.

"Let's see," I said. "What's the freshest fruit?"

"Blueberries," said the figure at the window. "Blueberries picked in a field at the height of summer, miles and miles and miles from anywhere this train will go."

"And how's your apple?" I asked.

"I can't get it into my mouth, not with a mask on."

"We have to wear these masks, though," I said. "It's because of water pressure."

"So they say."

"Or maybe it's salt lung, or seaweed breath."

"Yes, they also say that."

"Of course, some say that wearing these masks is just a superstition, left over from the old myths."

"Then why are you wearing one?"

"To disguise my identity," I said. "How about you?"

"The same reason."

"I don't think it's working," I said.

"Your disguise isn't working either. I knew the moment you walked in here that you were Lemony Snicket."

I took the mask off. It didn't affect my breathing. Still, I felt as if I were in danger of drowning, or at least swimming in waters that were perilous in some way. "Perilous" means dangerous. If you are in a room with a perilous person, you should leave it. I stood there in the room looking at the figure who was removing a mask and facing me. "And I knew," I said, "from the moment that I walked in, that you were Ellington Feint."

CHAPTER EIGHT

Ellington stood up, and we stood together unmasked, thinking about each other. The world continued to rotate. I'd learned long ago, as everybody learns, that the earth turns around something called an axis, which is a word for a line that goes down the middle of something. It's not a real line. The axis is imaginary, a line that exists only in your mind. I had never understood it until that moment in the train compartment. Ellington Feint was a line in my mind running right down the middle of my life, separating the formal training of my childhood and the territory of the rest of my days. She was an axis, and at that moment, and for many moments afterward, my entire world revolved around her.

"Hello," I said.

"Same to you," she said. "How did you find me?"

"This is the only place on the train where you can find coffee," I said, and showed her the tiny folded cup. She raised her curious eyebrows, shaped like question marks, and finally gave me the smile she always gave me, the smile that could have meant anything. "That looks like the work of Ornette Lost," she said.

"I suspect she's on board."

If Ellington was surprised, she did not show it. She reached underneath the table and retrieved a dark green bag I recognized at once. It was tube-shaped and had a secret compartment that had held a book called *Caviar: Salty Jewel of the Tasty Sea*, and the book in turn held a secret. But the book was gone now, and Ellington glanced at me and then reached in and tugged at a smooth black panel in the bag, and from under the false bottom she retrieved something that looked like a glass pitcher, with some kind of metal pump on the top and a sieve that fitted perfectly in the middle of the thing.

"What is that?" I asked her.

"This," she said, "is one of the greatest inventions mankind has ever known. It's called a French press, and it'll make much better coffee than that slop over there. I'll show you."

She showed me. She found an electric kettle and plugged it in, and then stood on tiptoe to take down a sack of coffee. She slid the pump out of the pitcher and poured in several handfuls of the ground coffee beans, almost as dark as her hair. The kettle steamed, and Ellington carefully poured hot water into the pitcher, onto the coffee, and balanced the pump on top of the pitcher but didn't lower it in.

"And now?" I asked.

"Now we wait," she said, and we sat at the small table. The water and the coffee mixed and clouded, like bad weather or troubled thoughts. She reached into a pocket of her rumpled clothing and brought out a small music box. She did not use the small crank to open the small panel that held a photograph I did not want to see, showing her missing father, a man with kind eyes and an open smile. She wound the crank the other way, and the music box began to sound out the small, melancholy tune I always remembered and never knew the name of. The song settled in the room, and we looked out the window at the darkness hurrying past. I put the little folded cup down between us and looked at its crinkly steam. I couldn't think of what to say, so I didn't say anything. I was not quite certain what I wanted to think about, so I tried not to think at all. I had no idea what to do, so nothing is what I did, as the sad tune played until it was over.

"Shall we talk now, Snicket?" she said, winding the crank again.

"Certainly," I said. "You could start by telling me why you're sitting in the Café Compartment, talking to me, when you should be locked in a cell in the prison car."

Her eyes watched me carefully. "You want to know about the prison car?"

"I want to know how you got out."

"The Mitchums let me out."

"Why would the Mitchums let you out?"

She looked away. "Out of the kindness of their hearts."

"Don't be absurd. The Mitchums may be less than perfect, but they wouldn't release a criminal from a cell."

She nodded. "Yes they would," she said, "if they thought something more important was at stake."

"Like murder?" I said.

Her eyes slid off mine and scuttled to the window. She wouldn't even meet my gaze when it was reflected in the window, but she still nodded a tiny nod.

"Dashiell Qwerty was a fine librarian," I said.

"I know he was," she said. Her body trembled in a small shudder that didn't look right, and she grasped the handle of the French press and lowered the pump until all of the coffee grounds were trapped at the bottom, separated from the coffee. "I guess a fine librarian is no match for a ruthless villain."

"Hangfire killed Qwerty?" I said.

"Of course," Ellington replied, and went to the counter to retrieve two cups. Ellington Feint had taught me to drink coffee but not to like it. Nobody can teach you how to like something. You can like it, or you can pretend to like it, in order to make someone happy. Of course, that other person might be pretending too, and so on and so on and so on, with all the world in a chain of pretense and distrust. "Who else would kill him?"

"Anyone in the Inhumane Society," I said. "Anyone who associates with Hangfire."

"I don't think Hangfire would trust anyone else to do something so important," she said, "or so treacherous."

"Hangfire lurks in the background," I reminded her, "imitating people's voices and making mysterious phone calls. He doesn't do anything himself."

Ellington poured the coffee. "Well, this time he did," she said. "He shot Qwerty with a poison dart and threw the weapon out the window. Then he slipped into a nearby compartment and frightened the librarians into serving as false witnesses."

She set a cup in front of me. I watched her through the steam. The song played on.

"What?" she asked.

"I don't like it," I said.

"You haven't tried it yet, Snicket."

"I don't mean French press coffee," I said. "I mean your story."

"What don't you like about it?"

"Maybe I don't like that you can calmly pour hot coffee while talking of cold-blooded murder. Maybe I don't like that I was in the corridor right after the murder, and there was no sign of anyone slipping into a nearby compartment. Or maybe I don't like the idea that Hangfire wasn't even on the train until a few minutes ago."

"Are you sure?"

"My associates saw a masked figure board the train when it stopped."

"A masked figure could have been anyone." She leaned over and blew on her coffee, sending the steam up into my eyes.

"Who else could it have been?"

"It could have been the person you least

suspect. Even the noblest of volunteers can associate with the wrong people."

"I can think of an example," I said, "sitting
right across from me."

It was dark outside, but the room felt darker
when she stood up. "What kind of villain do you
think I am?" she said, her eyes desperate and
blinking fast.

"I think you've helped the worst sort of villain," I said. "Hangfire has quite the menu of
misdeeds. He framed Qwerty for arson and
Theodora for murder. He's done everything he
could to stop Cleo Knight from finishing her formula for invisible ink, a formula that might save
Stain'd-by-the-Sea once and for all. He has a horde
of schoolchildren at his mercy at Wade Academy, stealing melons from Partial Foods. He's
destroyed libraries and schools and every piece of
evidence that might give away his scheme."

"You're the one who got that book destroyed,"
Ellington said. "I was trying to keep it safe, and

169

you wrecked my plan. You've wrecked every plan since you've set foot in this town. Maybe I'm wrong about what kind of person you are, Snicket. And maybe you're wrong about who Hangfire is."

"I hope I am," I said, "because I think you're waiting in this Café Compartment to give him the last crucial item he needs for his plan."

"I don't have the Bombinating Beast," she said wearily. "It was confiscated at Wade Academy. If Hangfire doesn't have it, I don't know who does. Search my bag again if you must."

She picked up the green tube and threw it to me, but I let it fall onto the floor with a heavy *thump* that rattled the compartment. "I don't need to search," I said. "I know you have that statue, Ellington. That's why Hangfire's on this train. That's why the bell's just rung again and everyone's in masks. The Bombinating Beast is the last thing he needs to complete his plan, and you're going to give it to him."

She knelt down to pick up the bag, and then leaned close to me. The song seemed to get sadder, and her eyes were very dark and very green. "You're wrong, Snicket," she said.

"I hope you're right about that," I said. "If Hangfire gets his hands on the Bombinating Beast, he'll probably kill you as surely as he killed Qwerty."

Ellington lowered her head. "He won't kill me," she said, very quietly. "Not after all I've done for him."

"Does it bother you, when you think about it?" I asked her. "Does it trouble you to think of all the things you've done since you arrived in this town?"

The tune had ended again, and Ellington picked up the music box and wound the crank, this time the other way. The photograph of her father fell into her hand. He was still smiling. I could not imagine what there was to smile about.

"Everything I did," Ellington said, "was to rescue this man. He's a kind man, Snicket. You'd like him."

"I'm sure I would," I said.

"He's a brilliant scientist. A naturalist like him could help save Stain'd-by-the-Sea."

"That's probably true," I said.

"And he's a wonderful father," she said. "He taught me everything I know."

"Everyone should have a wonderful father," I said.

"Then you understand why I want him back, Snicket. And you promised to help me. Remember?"

"Yes," I said, "but I didn't promise to like it," and I took a sip of coffee. It felt very heavy and very strong, like the darkness rushing by outside the window. In that darkness, I knew, beyond the reach of the law, was the vast expanse of the Clusterous Forest, full of shivering secrets that might never come to light. The coffee was like those strange, unknown secrets, a shuddering darkness inside me, but I kept drinking more and more.

Someone else dies, in this account. You might as well know that now, before you think to continue. Someone dies, and it is my fault. I wish I could say I was sorry about it, but all I can manage is that I'm sorry I'm not sorry, which is a sorry state of affairs.

"Do you like it now?" Ellington asked me, after a long pause.

"No," I said.

"I don't mean the story," she said. "I mean the coffee."

"No," I said.

"I'm sorry to hear that," she said.

"Why?"

"I'll be honest with you," she said, and hesitated. "I have a feeling this is our last time together."

"I hope not," I said. "I hope we know each other forever, and I hope we travel farther than this.

There are many wonderful places, Ellington—places we'll like better than Stain'd-by-the-Sea. I hope we see them together."

She finished her cup. "Why do you want to see those places with me?"

"Because I enjoy your company," I said.

"But why?" she said. "That's the mystery I can't figure out, Snicket. Why would you associate with me, after all I've done? Why would you help me?"

I never got to tell Ellington Feint the answer to that question, although she gasped, right then, a sharp, sudden gasp, so sharp and so sudden that for a moment I thought I'd given her an answer that had shocked her. But I was wrong. She hadn't gasped because of anything I'd said. The reason for her gasp was the same as the reason she stood up. It was the same as the reason she clutched her hands, first one and then both, to her throat, dropping the music box to the table, where it broke to pieces and sent the photograph of her father drifting down to the carpet. It was the reason she stumbled back into her chair and then off the chair to fall limp to the floor. The reason was in her hand. I saw it as each finger fell open, one by one, each with a fingernail painted as dark and shiny as her hair as it fell over her face like a shroud. It was a poison dart, fired by the man who was standing behind me.

CHAPTER NINE

For the second time since I'd left the Far East Suite, death was in the room with me. I could feel it reaching hungrily toward me, from the masked man in the gray suit. I could not see his eyes behind his mask, but I felt them gazing at me as I knelt by the body of Ellington Feint. I pressed two fingers to her neck, just where it met her chin. It is the best place to feel a pulse. "Pulse" is a word for the throb of blood as it moves through someone's veins. It has a certain rhythm, like a tune that is played, in one way or another, by every living creature. I could not look at Ellington as I checked for it. My eyes fell instead on one of the legs of the small table. It was scarred with scratches and small holes.

"She's dead," I said finally, and covered her with my jacket. Hangfire didn't move. He was good. He had waited until the right moment to sneak into the compartment. Perhaps it had been when Ellington had thrown her bag. The *thump* might have covered whatever tiny noises he made at the latch of the door. It should not have surprised me that he had managed to do this. He had managed to do many devious things in the short time I'd known him. But I was surprised that he was just standing there, instead of slipping back out of the compartment or walking toward me. He had the dart gun in his gloved hands, but it wasn't even pointed in my direction. Perhaps it had no more darts in it. I couldn't tell.

"Lemony Snicket," he said finally. "At last we meet."

His voice sounded like nothing. It was perhaps a little tired, as if he had imitated so many other voices that he could no longer remember what he really sounded like.

"We've met before," I said. "We met at the Sallis mansion, when you were posing as a butler. We spoke on the phone at the Lost Arms. We talked in Colonel Colophon's room at the Colophon Clinic, and outside the Department of Education. And there have probably been other times, haven't there? You've been right where I was, nearby or even right next to me, and I didn't even know it."

He gave me a slow, small shrug. Villainy, I thought to myself, despite all the myths and fairy tales, despite all the stories in books and all the articles in newspapers, is not very mysterious at all. It is a person in a room. You've probably been in such a room yourself, and didn't know you were in the presence of a villain. It is even possible you were alone in that room, and all the while had no idea that villainy was hiding there.

"I suppose you want to know why I killed her," Hangfire said.

"I know why you killed her," I said. "You had no more use for Ellington Feint. She helped you steal. She helped you kidnap. She helped you murder. And then your plan was through, and you were through with her. You forced her to do so many villainous things, and she never even knew exactly who she was helping."

"I never forced her," Hangfire said. "No one can force Ellington Feint to do anything. I just gave her a push in the right direction. A human being is like any other animal, Snicket. If it wants something enough, it will do anything at all."

The way he said *it* felt very wrong, like Ellington pouring coffee and talking about murder. "Ellington Feint," I said, "wanted to see her father again."

"The world is full of disappointment," he said, and sat down on the bench. He had terrible posture, I noticed. Something had hunched him over, like a storm can ravage a tree. He looked down at the weapon in his hands, cradling it like a sleepy infant. "Do you know what the poison is made of?" he asked, almost to himself.

"That's the wrong question," I told him.

"Not at all," Hangfire said, with a shake of his mask. "You can't know the ending of a story unless you know how it begins. When this land was covered in water, a certain seaweed flourished, spreading its sticky stems and tiny flowers across the seafloor. The scent of the flowers attracted schools of tiny fish who knew how to eat the flowers without getting stuck on the stems. When Ink Inc. drained the sea away, the fish all perished, but the seaweed kept growing."

"The Clusterous Forest," I said, with a glance

out the window. "The train is approaching that terrible place."

"It's not so terrible," Hangfire said. "It's simply a collection of plants that somehow found a way to survive. I spent a great deal of time there, learning the way of the lawless world. Even with the sea gone, the seaweed still grows flowers, and the flowers now attract a tiny bird, no bigger than that music box." He pointed a gloved finger at the broken machinery on the table. "The trouble is, the birds never learned the fishes' secret. They stand on the stems, and after eating the flowers they can't fly away. They stick, bird after bird, and they stay stuck. The birds starve, Snicket. After a few weeks you can see their bare skeletons still clinging to the seaweed. It is not difficult to pluck the skeletons off, and to grind the bones to a fine powder. If you mix this powder with milk, you have a powerful poison."

"That's a charming story," I said. "You should put it into a book for toddlers."

Hangfire gave me the sigh that adults sigh at children all over the world. "You're missing the point," he said. "Do you think the birds are the victims of a terrible plot? Are the stems of the seaweed villainous? Are the tiny fish to blame for this grave situation, because they never learned to live without water? Of course not, Snicket. Each creature is simply trying to get what it wants, and to make its way through a difficult world."

I sat and looked at him. I sat and wished that what he said made no sense.

"For years, I spent my days watching nature," Hangfire said, "and when the trouble began in Stain'd-by-the-Sea, I lowered my eyes to the sea. I watched the behavior of the denizens of the deep, and I stepped outside the law to get what I wanted. A denizen, by the way, is a creature that belongs where it lives."

"I know what 'denizen' means," I said.

Here Hangfire chuckled. "Of course you do.

You spend all your time in libraries, ignoring what's going on in the outside world."

"I know what happened just outside the library in Stain'd-by-the-Sea," I retorted. "I read all about it, Hangfire. You and your comrades rigged an explosion during the groundbreaking ceremony for the statue in honor of Colonel Colophon. That was the beginning of the Inhumane Society, wasn't it? Since then, you've been lurking in the shadows and plotting against the good people of Stain'd-by-the-Sea."

"Good people?" Hangfire repeated. "Are you sure about that, Snicket? Would good people chop down a tree that was hundreds of years old, to erect a statue in honor of bloodshed? Would good people drain the sea, just so they could force ink out of the last few octopi? What do you think happened to the water that drained away? A whole valley was flooded. Countless creatures of Killdeer Fields were drowned, and an entire village was forced to leave their homes, just so the Knight family could add a few pennies to their ink fortune and the town could limp along for a little while longer."

"But you're putting a stop to all that," I said. "You've tricked people into helping this town destroy itself, haven't you? Sally Murphy, Dr. Flammarion, Nurse Dander, Sharon Haines, Ellington Feint and her father—they all did their part to shut down Stain'd-by-the-Sea for good. They didn't always know what they were doing, any more than the schoolchildren at the Wade Academy know their part in your plan, and when they're no longer of use, you get rid of them. But thanks to them, there will be no more books, no more newspapers, no more libraries, and no more librarians. When your plan is completed, we'll all be denizens of the natural, lawless world. Is that about right?"

Hangfire didn't answer. He still had the dart gun in his hand, but it was pointed downward, as if the whole thing were none of his concern.

185

So I slowly picked up Ellington's bag from the floor and watched his eyes widen in the mask. I handed him the tube and he fell upon it like a predator.

"The Bombinating Beast," he said, in the wildest voice I'd heard from him, but when he unzipped the bag and stared into it, he didn't say anything.

"It's not there, Hangfire," I told him. "You killed Ellington for nothing."

"She betrayed me," Hangfire said softly. I watched the bag shiver in his hands.

"Maybe," I said.

"Where is it?" he asked.

"That's what you've asked yourself, over and over," I said. "Isn't that right, Hangfire? That's the question you've asked yourself all those days and nights. You lurked in the shadows, thinking of the old myths and superstitions. Night after night you dreamed of this scheme, you and your associates in the Inhumane Society. You hid at

Colophon Clinic, and you hid at Wade Academy. You rang the bell at Offshore Island, and you committed theft, and kidnapping, and arson, and murder. And night after night you were disappointed, without that statue in your grasp. But tonight will be different, won't it?"

Hangfire asked the question that is printed on the cover of this book.

"Because tonight your scheme finally comes to an end," I said.

Hangfire gave a small, wheezy laugh from behind his mask. "You and your little army of volunteers will boldly and bravely capture me and turn me over to the authorities when this train reaches the city, and I'll spend the rest of my days as a denizen of prison while you repair the world. Is that about right?"

"That's exactly wrong," I said. "You've concocted a beautiful plan, Hangfire. I'm not going to mangle it."

He turned his mask to me. "But V.F.D. stands

187

for the true human tradition of justice and literature," he said. "I thought you'd find a lawless world an ugly place."

"It is ugly," I said, and laughed unpleasantly. "So is the carpet in this compartment. But I'm not going to fix it. Listen, Hangfire. Stain'd-by-the-Sea hasn't done me any favors. I've had nothing but trouble since the day I arrived, and I'll suffer no more of it. I've got a sister in jail and a suitcase full of books I've been meaning to read at the train station in the city. The world is beyond repair, and I'm not going to muck around in a miserable town trying to throw together some justice."

"I'm confused," Hangfire said, but he sounded more confused than that.

"It is confusing," I agreed. "Ellington Feint said she'd do anything and everything to get her father out of your clutches. She managed to steal that statue and keep it hidden, biding her time until she could exchange it for her father's

188

freedom. But maybe she did betray you. Maybe she doesn't have it anymore. Maybe she gave it to somebody, a friend, perhaps, for safekeeping."

Lying does not come naturally to me, not lying of this sort. I had to keep my voice steady, and my eyes locked with Hangfire's masked and blinking eyes. And I had to look like I might be lying. I couldn't look like I couldn't possibly be lying, because what kind of people look like that?

"You're lying," he said, with a dismissive wave of his glove, "just like all the others. I noticed some black cardboard went missing, and then suddenly your friends started offering me the statue. I suppose that firefighting niece made some decoys."

"This is no decoy," I said. "I have the real thing—the statue made of dark wood, with hollow eyes and a little slit on the bottom covered in crinkly paper."

"It won't do you any good," Hangfire said. "You don't know how to use it."

"I'm not interested in using it," I said, "except as something to trade. Ellington was going to trade it for her father. I'm going to trade it for my chaperone. I'll give you the statue and you'll make sure Theodora goes free."

"Theodora?" Hangfire repeated in astonishment. "You're trading the Bombinating Beast for the freedom of that ridiculous woman?"

"Ridiculous or not, that is my offer."

"I don't have to take offers from a child," Hangfire said, and gestured with his dart gun. "I could just take the statue and leave you dead on the ground."

"But you can't find it," I reminded him.

"Maybe I'll just tear this train apart," Hangfire said. "I have a number of associates here who can make sure I get my hands on it, and that everyone who knows its secret is slain."

"I have associates here, too," I said. "And you can't kill everyone who knows your secret. Quite a few people have read *Caviar: Salty Jewel of the Tasty Sea*."

"You haven't," Hangfire said. "It burned to ashes before you could finish it."

"I didn't need to read it," I said. "I don't need to discover the secrets in the book or in the statue. I don't care what your scheme is, exactly. I just want Theodora out of Cell Two. Do we have a deal?"

Hangfire lifted one hand, and for a moment I thought he was going to remove his mask. But he simply took off one glove, finger by finger, and shook my hand. He had a very good handshake, strong and solid. I made mine better when I felt his.

"We'll leave separately," I said, "and meet shortly in the Officers' Lounge. I'll give you the statue and you'll let Theodora out of the prison car."

"How will I do that?"

191

"I'm sure Stew Mitchum can convince his parents to help you," I said. "He's the one who got Theodora locked up in the first place."

"We'd better hurry," Hangfire said, and pointed out the window. "Soon *The Thistle of the Valley* will be in lawless territory."

"I'll go fetch the statue," I said, "as soon as you're gone."

Hangfire nodded, and then looked down at Ellington Feint, under my coat. "What should we do about *that*?"

"*That?*" I repeated. "*That*'s not our problem, is it?"

He stared at her for another moment. "I didn't want to kill her, you know," he said.

"I understand," I said. "You're a human being, and a human being is like any other animal. If it wants something enough, it will do anything and everything."

He nodded and regloved his hand before

unlatching the door. "I've underestimated you, Snicket."

I looked at him. "Yes, you have," I said, and he went out. I listened to the sound of my own breath, heavy and quick, as if I'd emerged from a deep dive into the ocean. I waited for a little while that felt long. The train rattled and heaved on its tracks, and turned a corner so even the pale rocks were gone in the dark. There was nothing out there now, absolutely nothing. I let nothing rush by, and then finally I knelt down and lifted my coat from the sprawled shape of the girl with black hair.

"You can get up now," I said, and Ellington opened her eyes.

CHAPTER TEN

She held out her hand and I lifted her up. It really was an ugly carpet, but the sight of Ellington Feint, alive and well, was anything but ugly.

"How did you know I was alive?" she asked.

"That's the wrong question," I said, remembering the rhythm of her pulse against my fingers. "The question is, why were you pretending to be dead?"

Ellington gave me a sly smile. "I saw Hangfire come in," she said, "but he fired the dart gun before I could say anything. The dart missed me by inches, landing right there, in the leg of the table. I thought quickly and fell to the ground with my hands on my neck. I managed to grab the dart on the way down, so it looked like he'd done as he'd planned."

"That's quite a trick," I said. "Do you really think you fooled him?"

"You fooled him too," she said. "It looks like he's going to free your chaperone."

"I had to think quickly," I said. "Tonight, we finally have an opportunity to defeat Hang-fire once and for all. There's only one person on this train who might stop us from stopping him."

"Who?"

"You."

She blinked her green eyes. "Me?"

I said "you" again.

"Why?"

"You know why. You've betrayed me, and

Stain'd-by-the-Sea, time and time again, to stand with Hangfire and his treachery."

She opened her mouth to say something and then shut it to stop saying it. The compartment rattled.

"But now you know just how wild and wicked Hangfire truly is. You said he wouldn't kill you, and look what he did. Hangfire tricks people into helping with his plan and then gets rid of them when he's done."

Ellington nodded sadly, and looked down at the carpet. The ruins of her father's music box, spilled in a small heap, did not make the carpet any less ugly. She leaned down and picked up the photograph. "My father's dead, isn't he?" she asked me. "Hangfire got rid of him. He sent Dr. Flammarion and Nurse Dander to jail. He threw Colonel Colophon out a window, and he drowned that actress in the basement. And when my father was of no more use to him, Hangfire killed him. Didn't he?"

"I'm not sure," I lied.

"I am," she said, and I watched a tear slide down her cheek as she looked at the man with the gentle smile. "He's probably been dead for a long time. Hangfire has been tricking me all along."

"The world is full of disappointment," I said.

"Yes," she said, "I heard him say that. And every creature is simply trying to get what it wants, and to make their way through a difficult world. Do you believe that?"

"No," I said. "There's more than that."

"Like what?"

"Like good books," I said, "and good people. And good librarians, who are almost both at once."

She gave me a smile so small and gentle that it made me lonely just to look at it. "With all due respect," she said, "you're a very strange young man, Lemony Snicket."

"Not really," I said. "I'm just someone who

wandered into town and found myself in a story full of treachery and trouble. I'm going to do what I can to stop it. You can join me, Ellington. You can join anyone who's trying to save Stain'd-by-the-Sea, instead of destroying it."

"Join V.F.D.?" Ellington said quietly. "They'd never associate with me. After what happened at the Wade Academy..." Her voice trailed off. My account of our time at the Wade Academy is enough to make anyone's voice trail off, which is why I do not recommend reading it.

"I would associate with you, Ellington," I said.

"Even after everything?"

"Even after everything."

Her green eyes searched me. "Why?" she said.

I looked away and thought of all the books she'd almost destroyed when the library flooded. I thought of the book next to my bed in the Far East Suite, which I would never finish, and the book about caviar that had burned to ashes, which I would never read, and I thought about the librarian who had given me both. "I want to know what happens next," I said.

She reached out to touch the French press. It was cool by now, and for a moment it looked like she was going to put it back in the secret compartment in her bag. "What does happen next?" she asked.

"Next we hide you," I said. "Hangfire thinks you are dead. We can't have you wandering around the train."

"That would be undesirable," she agreed. "Can your associates hide me?"

"I don't want them to know you're out of your cell," I said.

"Why not?"

"They won't trust you."

"Even if I'm with you?" she asked.

I shook my head. "Even the noblest of volunteers can associate with the wrong people."

She blinked at me. "Do you really think I could join V.F.D. when this is all over?"

"If you help us defeat Hangfire," I said, "you will already have joined."

She pointed at my ankle. "Will it be absolutely necessary to get a tattoo like yours?"

"Moxie made us some business cards," I said, "that seem to be working well enough. Come on, grab your French press and we'll get out of here."

Ellington put her bag on her shoulder. "Forget the press," she said. "Tell me, Snicket, what makes you so sure you tricked Hangfire, and didn't get tricked yourself?"

I looked at the bag. I could have searched it. She'd challenged me to search it. "With all due respect," I said, adopting an expression she'd used that would always make me think of her, "that's the wrong question."

"What's the right one?"

I handed her one mask and lowered the other

one over myself, and masked, we left the Café Compartment. "The right one is, where are we going?"

"And where *are* we going?" she asked.

"To the scene of the crime," I said, and led her back down the train, through sliding doors which rattled as we went through. A few passengers passed us by, their masked faces strange and impossible to read. We passed the librarians' compartment and then Sally Murphy's. We passed the compartment where I had found Kellar, and Moxie's, where my associates were waiting, and finally we arrived at the sliding doors to the prison car. I peered through to check for the Officers Mitchum, but they were nowhere to be seen. That wasn't why I had stopped.

"Locked," I said.

"Are you sure?"

I shook them to show her. "We've got to get in there," I said. "You've got to be hidden before my associates come out of the compartment, or

Hangfire approaches the Officers' Lounge to meet me."

"Surely you know how to pick a lock," she said.

"Do you have a hairpin?" I said. "A nail file? Do you have anything at all that might do the trick?"

Ellington was still masked, so I couldn't read her expression as she took her bag off her shoulder. She unzipped it and then there was a small object in her slender fingers.

"I thought so," I said.

"I thought you thought so," she said, and unlocked the door.

"Is there anything else in that bag you want to show me?"

"You can see for yourself," Ellington said, tucking the key back into the bag's secret compartment. "I don't have the statue, Snicket. What will you do when you meet Hangfire in the Officers' Lounge?"

"We'll find out," I said, and we went in. The prison car was rattly but empty, with one cell door open and the other closed, and the irritating lettering on the door in the back where Hangfire and I would soon rendezvous. "Rendezvous" is just a fancy word for "meet." There are others. Don't think about them. Don't think about anything, Snicket. Keep going. You have to be certain.

Cell One was windy and noisy and very cold. After recent events, I almost expected Qwerty to be alive and well, having played dead even better than Ellington had. It would have been nice to see him. But Qwerty was not in the compartment. I looked around the empty cell and then at Ellington. She's a box of fire, I thought. You cannot keep her near you for long, but there is no safe place to stow her away.

Ellington turned her mask to look at me. "I'm going to hide here?"

"You're going to hide where the killer hid,"

I said, and stepped carefully across the broken glass and leaned out the window. The black air rushed by. "All of us rushed into the compartment and found Qwerty murdered, but nobody thought to look out the window."

She stood next to me and peered out of the shattered hole. "The railing looks decorative," she said. "It won't support my weight."

"It supported mine," I said, and unclipped my belt, "and when I was nine years old, I learned how to fashion a makeshift harness from a strong belt. It would be a shame to waste that expertise."

"You know what else would be a shame?" she asked. Even through the mask's filter I could hear the tremble in her voice. "Falling off a speeding train."

"It would be a shame," I agreed, "but it's not going to happen."

"There must be another place to hide." Her eyes blinked very fast behind her mask. "The

Mitchums let me out of my cell. Maybe they'll hide me, too."

"It won't work," I said. "The Mitchums will tell Stew, and Stew will tell Hangfire."

"I'm not going out there."

"People all over the world, in every age in history, have done daring, impossible things for more or less noble reasons. Your turn now, Ellington."

"I won't do it. Please, Snicket. I'm *scared*!" Her voice rose over the sound of the wind, and I shivered in the broken cell.

"Get scared later," I told her. "I'll take you to those wonderful places I told you about, and you can get scared then."

She took a step toward me, clasping the bag tightly. I wrapped the belt crisscross around her and started a Devil's Tongue knot, which had never failed me. "Tell me about the places," she said, as I worked on the harness.

"Winnipeg is supposed to be lovely this time of year," I said.

"Winnipeg?"

"It's at the confluence of two large rivers that turn gray and still at night," I said. "Winnipeg has been greatly influenced by French culture, so it will be no chore at all to find a good French press. We will drink coffee and watch the river from the balcony of the house of an associate of mine. We will attend masked balls at her castle, and you can get scared then."

"Castle?" she said.

"My associate is the Duchess of Winnipeg," I said, "or she will be, when her mother dies."

"My father is already dead," she said.

"Don't think about him," I said, and I reached out my hand. Ellington grasped it, and together we stepped onto the little table by the window. The wind rustled through us. She held on tightly to me, and I could feel how frightened she was.

"It's important, Snicket," she said, and she had to raise her voice now that we were so close to the clattering night. "It's very important that you come back for me."

"I think that every time you go away," I told her, and lowered her down. I double-knotted the belt to the railing. Then I triple-knotted it. Then I triple-checked it. And then I let go. I could see her dimly in the dark, a masked bundle tied to the side of the train, like some trapped orphan in a wicked book. She might have been quiet, or perhaps she was screaming. I couldn't hear anything but the noise of the train. Dear Kit, show me a man who dangles a girl from a train and I will show you a villain. Are you, I asked myself. Are you a villain? You are part of a noble organization. You have noble associates on the train, and those are just the ones you know about. Together you will defeat the treachery of the devious man and solve the murder of the noble one. It will be a triumph of libraries over treachery. The town will cease to be tormented by the myth of the Bombinating Beast, and the world will be quiet again, and the volunteers will gather around a table and feast on good food in celebration of a new formula for invisible ink that will restore the town of Stain'd-by-the-Sea. You're not a villain. Are you?

No one answered. It wasn't really the kind of question that gets an answer, which was too bad, because I wanted one. So I had to answer myself. Keep going, Snicket. You must be certain, because you might be wrong. You might be wrong about all of it. You could burn down a whole glyptotheca and not find the statue you wanted to steal. You might be wrong, so you must be certain, and the way to be certain is to dangle the frightened girl from the speeding train. It is a relief, Snicket, how frightened she is. It means she's never done it before.

CHAPTER ELEVEN

It was an empty journey out of the prison car. There wasn't a sign of anyone and out the windows was nothing but night and noise. The train whistle blew and I thought of my early bedtime, and the lonely sound I heard from my bed in the Far East Suite that began this journey. I wondered where it would end.

I let myself into Moxie's compartment, my thoughts as dark as the view outside, and for a moment I felt like an intruder, intruding on my favorite kind of gathering. Masks and coats had been piled into a corner and everyone was quiet and focused on the task at hand. Here and there on the carpet were crumpled-up pieces of paper, tossed away when something hadn't been figured right, and there were neat stacks of typed pages lined up on the bench, when something had been figured out exactly. And doing the figuring were all my associates from Stain'd-by-the-Sea, Moxie Mallahan and Kellar Haines at the typewriter, Jake Hix and Cleo Knight standing over the notes with Ornette Lost, who was the first to look up at my arrival, her eyes bright and cautious under her cap.

"Lemony Snicket," she said. "Surprised to see me?"

"I knew you were on board," I said, as the others gathered around. Jake clapped me on the shoulder, and Moxie gave me a hug I wasn't sure I deserved.

"You're back," she said. "You're back, and you're safe."

I tried to return her smile, and gestured to the typed pages. "Dashiell Qwerty would be proud to see this."

"We've been working hard comparing notes," Moxie said, "but what about you, Snicket? Have you learned anything while you were away?"

It was a question my parents always asked when I walked in the door, and for a moment I wondered if I would ever hear it again. "I hope so," I said, and moved a stack of paper so I could sit down. The two cardboard statues were busy being paperweights, and I reached into my pocket for another of Ornette's paper sculptures, the folded cup with the crinkly steam.

"You found my message," Ornette said with a smile. "The others were sure you would."

"Ornette had Pip and Squeak taxi her to Off-shore Island," Kellar explained, "and she snuck aboard when the train stopped."

215

"I'm the one who made the beasts," Ornette said. "If I hadn't made two of them, Hangfire never would have realized what we were up to. I'm responsible for the mess we're in."

"Kellar and I are responsible," Moxie said. "We each cooked up the same plan."

"We're *all* responsible," Cleo said. "If my formula was done, we wouldn't worry about Hangfire's mess."

"I knew I had to warn everyone," Ornette said, "but I was caught sneaking aboard."

"Who caught you?" I asked.

"Two people who said they were real live train conductors."

"Gifford and Ghede," Kellar said, frowning over his notes.

"I managed to distract them," said Ornette, whose powers of distraction had helped us before, "and I left a message on the floor. I saw a masked figure enter the Café Compartment, before the bell even rang. I figured it was Hangfire."

Everyone turned to me. "Was it Hangfire?" Moxie asked quietly. "Did you find him?"

"He found me," I said.

Moxie straightened her hat and went to her typewriter, flexing her fingers like a pianist or someone who handles poisonous snakes. "Tell us everything," she said.

"Well, first I had some coffee."

Moxie narrowed her eyes at me. "There's only one person who would make you drink coffee, Snicket."

"Ellington Feint made me a cup with a device she brought with her," I admitted.

Jake gasped. "How did that girl get out of her cell?"

"It wasn't much of a cell," I said, "not with the window shattered."

"Ellington Feint and Dashiell Qwerty shared Cell One," Moxie said, typing it as she realized it, and then she stopped and looked at me. "She must have killed him."

217

I thought of Ellington dangling out the window of the train, and shook my head.

"I know how you feel about Feint," Cleo said to me. "We all do, Snicket. But if Theodora is not the murderer, then Ellington Feint must be. There was no one else in the compartment."

"I didn't see anyone else," I said. "That's not quite the same thing."

Kellar looked around the room. "There aren't too many places to hide in these compartments," he said thoughtfully. "I suppose you could duck down under the table, or curl up in one of the racks."

I shook my head. "Someone would have noticed," I said.

"Maybe the killer ran out of the compartment before anyone else arrived," Ornette said.

I shook my head at her, too. "The Mitchums were coming from the Officers' Lounge," I said, "and I was coming from the opposite direction. Somebody would have seen the murderer."

"But nobody did," Moxie said.

"Well, it can't have happened like those so-called witnesses told it," Jake said sourly.

"I talked to those three myself," I said. "They're librarians, and they're scared. They witnessed something, all right. But it wasn't Qwerty's murder." I sighed, and looked at all the shared research. "Dashiell Qwerty was a noble librarian, working with us on a volunteer basis. He recommended book after book until I uncovered the sinister mystery that surrounded me, and saw the entire story of this town. The Inhumane Society realized this, and framed Dashiell Qwerty for arson to get him out of town. My chaperone had a plan to set him free, by disguising herself as a train conductor and sneaking him out of his cell. Qwerty wanted to stay on board so he might warn others in the city about Hangfire's plans. He was murdered in the middle of their argument."

"So Hangfire killed Qwerty?" Jake asked. "That scoundrel will stop at nothing."

"It would have been impossible for an adult to commit the crime," I said, "even an adult scoundrel. Qwerty was killed from outside the train, by a person hanging on to the railing. An adult would have been too heavy to hang on to the outside of the train. The killer was a child."

"So it *was* Ellington Feint," Moxie said.

I shook my head again. "Ellington didn't commit the crime, but she witnessed it. When the Mitchums arrived on the scene, she traded her freedom for her silence about the killer. The officers granted her freedom, and hid her in the Officers' Lounge while they covered up for the crime."

"Why would they do that?" Cleo asked. "Why would they cover up a murder?"

"I'm sure it was heartbreaking," I said, "for the law to do something so lawless. But they were protecting someone important to them— their darling little boy. It was Stew Mitchum who clung to the railings of *The Thistle of the*

Valley, shot Dashiell Qwerty with a poison dart, and then escaped into a compartment full of librarians scared into hiding the truth."

"He must have passed right by our window," Moxie said with a shudder, looking out at the blackness.

"So Theodora *was* railroaded," Kellar said, "and is locked in Cell Two for a crime she didn't commit."

"Tonight," I said, "we're going to get her out."

Everyone looked at me. "How are we going to do that?" Jake asked me.

"The Mitchums aren't going to let her out of there," Moxie said. "They helped frame her for murder to protect their son."

"They'll let her out if Hangfire tells them to," I said.

"And why would Hangfire tell them to?" Cleo asked.

I picked up a cardboard paperweight. "In exchange for the Bombinating Beast."

Kellar frowned. "But that's the wrong plan," he said. "Hangfire received too many messages, so he knows our statue is a decoy."

Moxie blinked, and I saw her hand reach for her typewriter and stop. "The real one," she said quietly. "The real statue. Ellington had it, last we knew. Did she give it to you?"

"She said it was confiscated a long time ago," I reminded her. "When we were at Wade Academy."

"No way, Fay Wray," Jake scoffed, using a favorite expression of his. "It wasn't true then and it isn't true now. If Hangfire had the Bombinating Beast, his plan would be complete."

"Did you search her bag, Snicket?" Cleo asked. "You told us it had a secret compartment."

"The only thing in that compartment," I said, "is a skeleton key."

"A skeleton key?" Kellar repeated incredulously. "She has my mother's skeleton key, and you still believe she isn't helping Hangfire?"

"I believe Hangfire would kill Ellington Feint if he could," I said with a shiver, "and Ellington knows it."

"And the beast?" Moxie asked. "Where's the statue, Snicket?"

"I don't know," I admitted, "but I promised Hangfire I'd bring it to him in the Officers' Lounge."

"When?" Cleo asked.

I looked around at all my associates and gave them a rueful smile, and "rueful" is a word which here means "not smiley." "Now," I said.

Jake shook his head. "This is a kettle of fish," he said, "and I don't mean the delicious kind."

Moxie was paging through another pile of notes. I spotted the word "aquarium," which is a difficult word to type. "Not fish," she said. "Tadpoles. Isn't that right, Snicket? Those tadpoles you saw when you were following Nurse Dander?"

I gave her a small shrug. "There's a lot I don't

223

know about the natural world," I said. "Hang-fire told me a ghastly story about the skeletons of birds in the Clusterous Forest."

I gestured at the dark view, and Ornette stepped to the window and put her hand on the glass. "I've never been this far," she said, "not since they built this part of the railway line."

Moxie followed her gaze. "From the seafloor, you can't see the light of the lighthouse at all," she said.

"In the dark, you can't see any of the ink-wells," Cleo said.

Then there was a rustle against the window of the compartment, and for a startling moment something pressed against the glass like it was trying to get in. The thing looked like a tiny tentacle, wet and sticky, and it left a faint, gleamy trail on the window when it disappeared. All of us jumped in surprise and then tried to look like we hadn't jumped in surprise, but Jake was the loudest at it.

"Egad!" Jake said. "What is that?"

Cleo put her hand on her sweetheart, with the same calm affection she always used with him. "It's seaweed," she said. "We must be on the edge of the Clusterous Forest."

I tried not to think of Ellington, and all of these strange tendrils bristling by as she hung on the railing. Tendrils are the smaller parts of plants, but they were large enough to make me shiver. I looked again at the little folded cup Ornette had made me.

"What is this?" I asked her.

Ornette frowned. "You know what it is," she said. "It's a cup."

"The cup is made from those black boxes of laudanum," I said, "and the saucer's made from one of your business cards. But what's the steam?"

"It's the same stuff we found around Wade Academy," Kellar said.

Ornette nodded. "And the same stuff you used on your hayride with Ellington."

"It's not hay," Cleo said, "and it's not sea-weed, or bark. This is what we've been working on, Snicket, quietly, without telling you or anyone else."

"There's a whole other mystery on this train," Jake said, "besides the death of Dashiell Qwerty."

Moxie was paging through her notes. "It's the story of the stolen aquarium equipment," she said, "and all those honeydew melons. Now that we've compared notes, we figured something out, and we think it's important."

"Is it the story of the drained sea and the statue outside the library?" I asked. "The story of Stain'd-by-the-Sea and the Inhumane Society?"

"Maybe it's the story of a little boy who finally got some sense knocked into him," said a wheezy voice from the doorway, and I turned to see the masked and unpleasant figure of Stew Mitchum. "Put your mask on, Snicket. You're coming with me."

"I don't have to come with you," I said firmly, "and I certainly don't have to put on my mask. The masks are just ancient superstition, and you're just as useless."

Stew stepped into the room. "Remember the beating I gave you in the alley?" he said, as if reminding me of a summer vacation instead of an incident described in a book I'm sure is of no interest to you.

Moxie stepped between us. "Last time my associate was in an alley," she told Stew, "he was alone."

Stew sneered. "Does little Lemon Snicker-doodle need a girl to protect him?"

"No," Moxie told Stew calmly. "But you might. We know what you did, Stew Mitchum. You're a murderer and you're going to jail for a long time."

"I'm no murderer," Stew said, "and I have three witnesses who proved it."

"Let's fetch those witnesses," Ornette said. "We have some more questions for them."

227

"And we'll fetch the authorities," Cleo said.

"You mean my parents," Stew said.

"We mean the law," Jake said.

Stew gestured to the seaweed sliding against the window. "My parents are only the law from the outskirts of Stain'd-by-the-Sea in the hinterlands to the boundary of the Clusterous Forest. We've passed that boundary now. We're in lawless territory, bookworms."

"The law's not the only authority on this train," I said.

Moxie clicked shut her typewriter case. "I'll get Gifford and Ghede," she said.

"I'll go with you," Kellar said, but I shook my head.

"Go find your sister," I told him. "She's safe, Kellar. She's in disguise, in a compartment just a few doors down."

Kellar's eyes widened, but his mouth couldn't decide whether or not to smile. "How did she get here?"

"With help from Sally Murphy," I said.

"You're lying," Stew growled. "Sally Murphy worked for us, until Hangfire took care of her."

"She's done with the Inhumane Society," I said. "She helped Lizzie escape Stain'd-by-the-Sea with some costumes and a thistle from Polly Partial. It's the performance of a lifetime, and so far she's doing a pretty good job of it. I only figured it was Lizzie when she said something I've only heard from Kellar. It must be a family expression, Haines. You'd better hurry up."

"I'm hurryupping," Kellar said hurryuppily, and he hurryupped out of the compartment without a word. The rest of my associates followed, leaving me alone in the compartment with Qwerty's murderer. "You have an appointment with Hangfire," he said. "Are you ready?"

I stole a look at the cardboard beasts, weighting down the stacks of notes. It was all those gimcracks were good for now.

I told him I was ready.

He led me down the corridor to the prison cars' sliding doors, which were propped open with an object he put into my hand.

"Wear this."

"The masks are just old superstition, Stew. I told you that."

"Hangfire has respect for the old superstitions," Stew said. "Put it on."

I put it on, breathing and buzzing. "It's a shame you have to use an old superstition to prop open the doors," I said. "A boy like you should have a good skeleton key."

Stew growled a little and pushed me through the doors. The corridor was empty, although the seaweed was slithering against these windows too, so my way to the prison car felt crowded and spooky. Stew's footsteps were loud behind me. I walked past the closed doors of both cells, which was a mistake, and stopped at the door of the Officers' Lounge. The lettering still irritated

me. Stew stepped to the door, and with a gesture like a bad actor, threw the door open, so
hard that it banged against its little doorstop
and threw itself back at us. It was not a graceful
entrance, but the person staring back at me was
not someone who cared about grace.

The Officers' Lounge was a shabby place,
with windows showing off the dark landscape,
a desk littered with official papers that were
probably as dull as they looked, and one lonely
lightbulb trying to illuminate the whole place. It
wasn't up to the job, and in an unlit corner was
a masked figure seated in a chair with carved
wooden legs. In the dim lounge I could see little
more than the shiny mask and the curved claws
that held up the chair. It was a disquieting sight,
a phrase which here means it made me uneasy
and silent, and for a moment there was only the
rattle of the train and the slithering of seaweed.

"Good evening," I said finally.

"It certainly is a good evening for us," Stew said, his sneer wheezy through the mask. "We've won, Snicket. Tonight we will finally be victorious over this rotten town. When you hand over the statue, Stain'd-by-the-Sea will be completely under the power of the Inhumane Society and the secrets we're cooking up at Wade Academy."

"There's nothing at Wade Academy," I said, "but a few dazed children and the remains of a top-drawer school. Hangfire's tricked you, Stew. He tricked everyone with a story of a mythical monster he's been keeping in a pond. With a little caviar sprinkled here and there, a few hungry tadpoles splashing in fishbowls, a heap of stolen melons, and an octopus or two scuffling in and out of a fire pond, you can have people believing anything."

"What I believe," Stew said, "is that you're going to give us the Bombinating Beast. I'll unlock Cell Two once I have the statue in my hands."

"Unlock it with what?" I said. "Ellington Feint has the only skeleton key around, and now she's used it to hide herself from the Inhumane Society."

"We'll find her soon enough," Stew said. "There aren't too many places to hide on board a train."

"That's true," I said, answering Stew but looking Hangfire right in the mask. Who else could it be, I thought, but it was too late. "It wasn't too difficult to find Lizzie Haines. Kellar is reuniting with his sister as we speak."

The figure rose from the chair and gasped a gasp that sounded wrong. Stew sputtered something, but the figure was already unmasking. The train lurched around a corner, and the rustle of seaweed ran along the walls and the ceiling as I blinked at what I saw.

I must have looked foolish, standing there gaping, so I suppose I can excuse Stew for his nasty giggle. I wasn't listening to him anyway. I was listening to the figure in the corner as she gasped again. I was wrong. Dread grew inside me, like a wild creature growing and thriving in some sinister place. Stew Mitchum was right. My brave words meant nothing, and there wasn't enough ink in the world to write down how very wrong I was. I'd been solving the wrong mystery. It was not Hangfire standing in the corner. He had found someone to do his bidding, someone who had lent a skeleton key first to my chaperone and then to Ellington Feint, in the hope that her daughter would be returned to her. The mask fell to the floor, and there stood Sharon Haines, another heartbroken parent, looking startled and sad.

"Where's Lizzie?" she asked me, and then turned to Stew. "You promised that if I boarded the train and pretended to be Hangfire, she would be set free. Where's Lizzie? Where is she?"

It was a good question, but it was wrong. The right question was "Where's Hangfire?" and I hurried out of the room to answer it.

CHAPTER TWELVE

I ran down the prison car. The seaweed was whispering at the windows, and the train lurched back and forth like it was as scared as I was. Dear Kit, since we were separated I've hardly done one single thing right. I miss you and I miss my brother and I miss my parents. Terrible things have happened while I was unsupervised. I thought I was a brave volunteer solving a case, but I am nothing more than a rat in a trap, a boy lost in a faraway land. Please come find me. I am

unmasked and breathless, standing in the doorway of Cell One for the last time.

It was the cell where Dashiell Qwerty had
been murdered, and where Ellington Feint
had bargained her way to freedom. It was the
cell where I'd hidden her away, but Ellington
Feint wasn't hiding anymore. She was no longer strapped to the outside railing of *The Thistle
of the Valley*, but had climbed back through the
window and was standing on the little table,
holding tightly to her green bag and still wearing her mask. She had not freed herself. She'd
had the help of the masked man in the gray
suit who was helping her now. They'd helped
each other before. He had fired a dart, and she
had lain on the floor pretending to be dead, in
order to trick someone. I thought I'd tricked
Hangfire, but now I saw, as he reached out a
gloved hand so she could step down and join
him, that I was wrong. He had tricked me. They
both had.

"Stop!" I cried. Their masks turned to face me as I stepped through the doorway, like two strange creatures interrupted in their native habitat.

"Snicket," both of them said in muffled, wheezy unison.

"Feint," I replied, and took one step closer to Ellington, but as I looked at her I could not think of a thing to say. I'd told her so many times that she shouldn't help Hangfire. I'd said she couldn't stand with the Inhumane Society and move their treacherous plot further along. Again and again I had said these things, and again and again Ellington had said she agreed with me. But it was a trick, I realized. She'd just wanted to push me in the right direction, and now it was too late.

"It's too late," she said.

"No," I said.

Hangfire helped Ellington to the ground. "The girl is right," he told me. "It is too late. You did your best, but it's all over for the people of Stain'd-by-the-Sea."

"It's too late for *you*," I said, as fiercely as I could, which was fiercer than I felt. "It's the end of the line, Hangfire. You and your organization will be arrested and stopped."

"No one will arrest me," Hangfire said, with a shake of his mask. "We're outside the boundaries of the law now, and at last I can find the justice I'm looking for."

"Destroying a town is not justice," I said. "Stealing is not justice. Kidnapping and arson aren't justice. And murder isn't justice!"

Ellington climbed down off the table, just as she'd climbed up the ladder the first night we'd met. She had saved me then. It was my turn. "If my father is returned to me," she said, "that's the justice I'm looking for. I can't stand with you, Snicket. You promised to help me, but you've brought me no closer to my father."

"Maybe you don't want to see him again," I said. "Maybe there are more important things."

She shook her head, and looked down at her hand. The photograph of her father was there, crumpled and slightly worn. "It's all I have," she said quietly.

"No," Hangfire said, and took a step closer to her. Tendrils of seaweed murmured at the broken window, and the villain's voice sounded just as wild and sinister, scarcely audible over the clatter of the train. "You have something else— something else you've promised me for too long. Now hand it over."

"She's already handed it over," said a voice from the doorway. My associates had arrived. Ornette was first through the door, her cap backward on her head and her hands balled up into fists. Cleo followed, with the folded cup in one hand and the hand of her sweetheart in the other. But it was Moxie who had spoken, and she stood in front of Hangfire with her typewriter in one hand and a statue in the other. "Ellington gave it to me," she told him. "That's why I sent you the message, Hangfire. I'm still prepared to exchange it."

"You fold together a flimsy decoy," Hangfire said scornfully, "and try to play me like a clarinet, but you'll collapse when you stand against me. All of you Stain'd citizens are the same. Your mother, Mallahan, was a journalist searching for the truth, but she didn't have the courage to face what she found. Your parents, Hix, are too scared to come back to town, even to fetch their son. The Knight family drained the sea, and then went down the drain themselves. I could go on and on. The Losts. The Bellerophons. Doctors and actors, nurses and naturalists. Everyone was utterly worthless, and then along came a little girl who could perform all the trickery I needed."

Hangfire turned his mask to Ellington,

and Ellington took off her mask and faced him directly. "Where's my father?" she asked him, and I saw her hands tremble as she took the bag off her shoulder. "What have you done with him? I've done everything you asked me to do, over and over again, but I won't hand over the statue until I see him."

"Don't make a bargain with a villain," I told her, as Hangfire stepped even closer.

"Give me the statue," Hangfire said, in a voice as whispery and frightening as the seaweed outside, "and you'll be side by side with your father before you know it."

Ellington looked at Hangfire, and she looked at me, and then she opened the bag and removed the small panel, then reached farther in and removed another panel. Underneath the secret compartment was a secret compartment, a trick hiding another trick. I stepped closer, and looked back at the doorway. It wasn't just my associates anymore. I saw Sharon Haines, and Sally

Murphy. I saw Lizzie Haines, still in her bearded disguise, and I saw Gifford and Ghede, still masked. I saw Stew Mitchum, and his parents standing nervously behind him, and I saw the three librarians taking careful note of everything that was happening.

I looked at Ellington, and Ellington backed away. Hangfire held out his hands to her, and Ellington's green eyes blinked at me one last time before she looked away and put a dark, dark object into the villain's gloves. It was about the size of a bottle of milk, but pitch black, with two small holes for the eyes and a few slits representing tiny, sharp teeth. At its base was another slit, patched with a piece of paper, and there were tiny scales here and there on its sides. It looked a bit like a sea horse, and a bit like a shark. It looked quite a bit like a nightmare. It was a statue of the Bombinating Beast, the dark figure of old myths and superstitions, and now it was in Hangfire's hands at last. The villain gazed down at it and

I heard a low, wild sound come from his throat, a hungry and desperate wheeze, like some wild animal within him was finally free and loose. Maybe you're happy now, Hangfire, I thought. Maybe you're as peaceful as you were before all this began.

Hangfire caressed the Bombinating Beast like it was his own flesh and blood, and then held it up like a weapon or a flag. He turned to face the crowd by the door, in a showy gesture I remembered from my schooling. There is always a show-off or two, in every classroom. Often it is the teacher, and when the teacher is showing off it is often the best time to do something sneaky.

"I have something to say," Hangfire announced. Nobody ever heard it. I had something to say, too. I did not face the crowd, but instead faced the broken window of the train, and pointed at it, too, to make it as obvious as possible.

"What's that behind you?" is what I said. It is a very old trick, perhaps the oldest one in the world. Like the old myths and superstitions, it almost always works. Hangfire turned his head, just for a second, and in that second I moved forward and snatched the statue from him. I moved quickly and strongly, and it made Hangfire stumble back against the table. The table made him stumble back against the bench. The bench made him stumble back against his own foot. His own foot made him fall to the floor, and the fall removed his mask and revealed his blinking, startled face. I didn't look at him. My eyes were on the Bombinating Beast, which shivered like a dark chill in my hands. Everyone else looked, though. Ellington looked hardest of all and gasped the loudest, over the gasps of everyone else and the unearthly sounds outside the broken window.

I looked back at the Mitchums. "Will you uphold the law?" I asked. "Will you arrest the criminals who are plaguing this town?"

Harvey and Mimi looked from Hangfire

to their son and then back at me. I waited but I didn't hope. They looked at me and quietly, barely, as I expected, shook their heads. At that moment I moved outside the boundaries of the law, just as *The Thistle of the Valley* had, and entered a wild, lawless place. I held the Bombinating Beast in my hands. It was why this night was different from all other nights.

I looked at the statue. It glared back at me like a wild creature, and I took a wild guess and brought it closer. I'd read the old myths in the library, in a book Dashiell Qwerty had given me. You could tame the Bombinating Beast by imitating its fearsome buzz. There was even a story of a wizard ordering the beast to do terrible things on his behalf, as long as it was kept fed.

I held the statue to my mouth, and then I simply breathed and kept still. The statue began to make a wheezy, buzzing sound, as my breath passed through the paper patch and was expelled through the slits and holes carved into its body. I played it like a clarinet, as had been suggested to me. It was not a loud sound, but even so I felt it go through the landscape like a scream. The sound did not fly out of the window and back toward town, across the ocean floor and up the rocky cliffs that had once overlooked the water. The sound did not clamber over the wall of the Wade Academy and stop short at the edge of the fire pond. It traveled in some other way, some way that science has not yet discovered. It moved the way an idea moves from a book to your mind, or the way strangers move together into friend-ship. It moved the way someone's very green eyes can move you to do something very wrong. It was wrong, very wrong, the wrong sound on the wrong night, and it reached the wrong place and the wrong ears, and the eyes it opened were wild and lawless.

The Bombinating Beast moved black and cold to the surface, and we froze and listened to it echo across the land and the sea, before Stain'd-by-the-Sea had occupied both. The sound moved deep underground, shivering and shimmering like something hidden, and then rattling and clattering, louder than the train. The Bombinating Beast lumbered out of the fire pond and over any wall foolish enough to try and contain it. It rushed unbound and unsupervised across the dark countryside the town had ruined. We could hear its tail lash out of the water and shake droplets into the sky. We could hear its claws across the ground, like sparks from a fire, and the rustle of its shiny, scaly skin against the helpless rocks, slithering past everything and making everything shudder. It galloped and swam, it leapt and it bounded. It moved like spilled ink across paper or dread across the heart. The Bombinating Beast moved like a heavy shadow, or an angry fist. It was enormous and slippery, desperate and hungry. It was coming closer. You could hear it over the train, buzzing toward us, ravenous and furious. The wind hurried from it with a sound of ripping paper, and the seaweed shrank back in the window as the vanished sea sensed its approach. Each leap of the beast was deep and thunderous, quicker and quicker like a terrified heartbeat. We cowered at the sound, all of us, and "cowered" means we closed our eyes and shook and clung to whatever we could with trembling hands.

I could not get scared later. I was scared right then.

The Bombinating Beast gave one great roar, deafening and reckless, and then it was upon us. There was a tremendous clang as it hit the train, and *The Thistle of the Valley* tumbled off the tracks and fell into the crackling seaweed of the Clusterous Forest. The room spun on its axis, all the way around, and all of us clattered against the walls and the floor. The compartment grew icy, and there was a great scuffling noise from the roof of the train, a rough slither like something dragged across the skin of the world. Then the beast appeared in the broken window.

The statue had not done the animal justice. Its teeth were sharper, and there were many more of them, clacking and gnashing at the air. Its mouth was soaked with slime and smelled of something buried long ago. Its eyes were fiery bright, fluttering with several sets of scaled eyelids moving like the blades of some infernal machine. Its skin shone with darkness, and seemed to be as wet as blood but as dry as the grave. And it was louder, louder than anything in nature, or inked into the paper of a book. We could only see its terrible scaly face, and one horrible clenched claw at the bottom of the window as it reached past the last broken shards of the glass toward us. Its forked tongue moved like a searching eel. It wanted something. It was hungry.

Only one person was brave enough to face the beast directly. He was a naturalist, after all. He was a scientist and a villain, curious and treacherous, and he stood and took one step toward it as it heaved and growled. He was not smiling, and he was not frowning. He looked content, as if something at last was his, as peaceful as he did in Ellington's photograph of him.

He was Hangfire, and Hangfire was Armstrong Feint.

"Father!" Ellington screamed, and the beast buzzed voraciously and the whole train shook. Ellington's father turned to face us and he pointed with one finger toward me. He was shouting something, but I could not hear what it was. There is often confusion regarding the last words of prominent individuals, a phrase which here means "heroes or villains." He stood in front of the mouth of the beast and shouted something, but even with three librarians present it was not recorded, and

those words have vanished. What I did has not vanished, even if I wish it were so. I stood up and did something Hangfire had done all over town.

I gave him a push in the right direction.

The villain fell away from his daughter and into the mouth of the Bombinating Beast. He was gone in no time at all. The teeth moved together, and there was the sound of a quick collapse, like something made of folded paper falling apart. A long, quick bulge appeared in the creature's throat, and then the forked tongue ran itself all over its teeth. Its unnatural eyes, dark and wet and blinking every which way, slid from me to the statue in my hands and back again. I didn't trust my voice. I just pointed, out the window, away from Stain'd-by-the-Sea and toward the depths of the Clusterous Forest. The beast buzzed again, and the whole train shook, like even the metal and the wood were quaking in fear, and then in one cold swoop it was gone. The seaweed rustled behind it and its noises faded in leaps and bounds. The buzzing stopped. It was quiet. Ellington was on the floor staring at me, her eyes frantic with grief and anger. She had words for me, but she couldn't say them. I didn't answer. I couldn't answer. I couldn't look at her. Around me everyone lay trembling and shivering on the ground. I let us tremble and shiver. For a moment there was nothing else to be done.

CHAPTER THIRTEEN

I heard noises around me, but I saw nothing.
I had closed my eyes without knowing it, the
way you can sometimes squint your way out of a
nightmare and find yourself safe in the morning
at last. What a strange and terrible dream you've
been having, I told myself desperately. I knew it
was nonsense.

I blinked my way back into the frightened
compartment. The statue was still in my hands,
but everything else was on the ugly carpet,

thrown there when the train had been driven off its tracks. My associates were scattered around the ruined room, and in a far corner was a heap of Mitchums beginning to disentangle themselves. Moxie was the first to sit up, reaching out an arm still scarred from an earlier case of ours, and retrieving her hat and her typewriter case. She blinked too, but she didn't look at me.

"What's the news, Moxie?" I said quietly, but she just shook her head and turned away. Her expression was grim, and her eyes looked dark and haunted, like the dead windows of so many buildings in town. I looked from her to the others, and everywhere it was the same. Friend or enemy, associate or stranger, they all shrank from me as I stepped out of the compartment into the corridor and disembarked from the train.

The Thistle of the Valley had been just at the edge of the Clusterous Forest, and the beast had knocked us back toward the empty landscape.

You could see the train spread out like a dead serpent. Some of the cargo cars were over-turned, and a few splashes of ink had spilled onto the ground in dark stains. I stepped through a few quivering tendrils and found myself on the empty, drained seafloor. The night still hung in the sky, but by the feeble light of the cres-cent moon I could see I wasn't the only person there. Other passengers were making their way off the train to stand in the eerie silence. Some looked hurt and some only looked scared. Some passengers were limping, and other passengers were helping them. Some people stood alone and some in little worried groups, some wearing masks and some who had discarded theirs. There were a few people who were very old, and a few infants held by their mothers and fathers. A few people looked slightly familiar, as if I had passed them sometime on the streets of Stain'd-by-the-Sea, but I didn't truly recognize anyone until I saw the Haines family stumble their way out of the seaweed, reunited and huddling together. Lizzie Haines, smiling faintly over her false beard, had one arm around Kellar and one arm around her mother, and behind the family came the nervous figure of Sally Murphy. I did not see the Mitchums, but Gifford and Ghede stumbled forward, still in their conductors' uniforms, guiding the three librarians, who stood in a cluster murmuring to one another. Lastly came my associates, those who had helped in my work and kept me company during my days in Stain'd-by-the-Sea: the chemist and the cook, the sculptor and the journalist, everyone but the one who had occupied my thoughts the most.

I didn't see Ellington Feint anywhere at all.

Over the eerie and dazed quiet I heard the sound of a familiar car engine, and a battered yellow taxi rattled into view. The Bellerophon brothers' taxicab looked like it'd had a very hard time following *The Thistle of the Valley*, and when

Pip rolled the window down, he looked as tired and battered as his automobile.

"This doesn't look good, does it?" Pip asked me, before anyone said hello. "Is anyone seriously hurt?"

I told him it sure didn't and I hoped not.

Squeak climbed up to face me. "What about you?" he asked. "Are you all right, Snicket?"

"Just the opposite," I said.

Pip frowned. "What was it, Snicket? What was that dark thing we saw?"

"It was something terrible," Squeak said. "We only got a quick look, but I had to remind my brother of what you said about getting scared later."

"You should probably stop listening to me," I said, but the people around us didn't appear to agree. They were stepping closer, circling around me as I stood by the taxicab talking.

"You know what happened?" asked a masked

woman holding a badly dented suitcase. "You know what that was?"

There was a murmur in the gathering crowd, and even the people I knew stepped toward me. "What's the story?" asked a man who was holding a handkerchief up to the cut on his face. A few drops of blood stained the handkerchief, and he grimaced a little, but not enough that he didn't look curious. Everyone did, and everyone waited, looking at me.

An instructor of mine once said that if you were nervous about speaking in front of a group of people, you should imagine them naked. He was standing in front of a large class when he said this, and we were not pleased to think that he was imagining us without our clothes on. I did not imagine the denizens of Stain'd-by-the-Sea without their clothes on, but as I stood in the empty landscape and cleared my throat, I did imagine them swimming, or trying to swim, right where we were standing.

"Let's begin at the beginning," I said. "Long ago, this entire area was covered in water."

People frowned at one another, and there were a few mutters here and there. "Look here, young man," Sally Murphy said. "I don't think we have to begin quite that far back."

"That's what I thought, too," I said. "I thought this story began when I arrived in town. I was wrong. It begins when Stain'd-by-the-Sea was a busy town, with bustling streets, a thriving ink industry, a well-regarded newspaper, and beautiful views of the sea."

"The town doesn't look like that anymore," Walleye said. "What happened?"

Cleo stepped forward, but wouldn't look me in the eye. "Plenty of things happened," she said. "It became harder to find octopi, so Ink Inc.'s ink became weaker and fainter. It made the articles in the newspaper seem less certain, and people who read it became uncertain themselves."

"They were upset that things weren't going

263

as well in the town," said Moxie, who wouldn't look at me either.

Jake nodded. "There was a war, and people argued whether Colonel Colophon was a hero, or just a violent man. Stores closed. Adults moved out of town and left their children behind. The police force shrank, and the library was almost forgotten."

"That's a rotten shame," Pocket muttered.

"There is nothing worse," Walleye agreed.

"Stain'd-by-the-Sea became a place of loneliness and discontent," I said, "so people took drastic action. They decided to drain the sea so the machines and the railways could find enough octopi to rescue the ink industry. It was a brave and unusual plan, and for a while it must have looked like it worked. But they were wrong. Draining the sea made things worse. It destroyed far more creatures than it uncovered, and it flooded the surrounding regions. Now there was more loneliness and discontent than ever."

"It's an old story," Eratosthenes said, stroking the ends of his beard. "I've heard versions of it before."

"But something began to feed on that loneliness and discontent," I said. "Something thrived on it, the way the seaweed of the Clusterous Forest thrives, even with the sea gone. A naturalist was distressed over what had been done to the sea and its creatures, and took inspiration from the wild and lawless ways of the untamed world, and from the old myths and superstitions that were around before Stain'd-by-the-Sea even existed. He gathered whatever associates he could find into an ad hoc organization."

"The Inhumane Society," Lizzie Haines said, so quietly that she probably didn't know she'd said it.

I nodded. "They banded together, and they got to work."

"They took an old tradition about ringing a gong and wearing masks," Moxie said, "and soon

265

had people cowering and disguising themselves whenever they needed to skulk around."

"They started fires," Kellar said.

"They set explosions, and they performed sinister experiments," Cleo said.

"They stole," Jake said, "and they kidnapped."

"They gathered associates and captured school-children. By the time I got into town, these people had been operating for quite some time. It took me a while to see that each mystery I encountered was part of a larger, treacherous plot. It's a fragmentary plot, a phrase which here means—"

"We know what it means," Walleye said. "It means that the treachery was scattered around, to various people."

"There's books with fragmentary plots too," Pocket said.

"Some say that the whole world is a fragmentary plot," Eratosthenes said.

"I haven't seen the whole world," I said, "but I've seen Stain'd-by-the-Sea. The treachery of the Inhumane Society was controlled by one man. As a brilliant scientist, he could have saved the town, but instead he fed on the loneliness and discontent of the fading town, and pushed people in the direction he thought was right. Sometimes he did it with laudanum, and sometimes he did it with hostages."

"Like Lizzie," Kellar said, and put a hand on his sister's shoulder. Sharon Haines looked at her children and then at the ground.

"Sometimes the people were willing to be wicked," I continued, "and sometimes they needed to be frightened into it. So the villain spread a frightening rumor, that a mythological creature was returning to Stain'd-by-the-Sea, a wild, lawless thing that could destroy the town once and for all."

"The Bombinating Beast," said a man in the crowd.

"You saw it for yourself," I said. "It's been around for a very long time, and so naturally there are wild and fantastic stories. But it's just an animal, trying to get what it wants, and to make its way through a difficult world. The underwater plants that hid the creature found a way to survive when the sea was drained away, but the Bombinating Beast needed a new home. Hangfire provided that home. He harvested the eggs in whatever damp places he could find. When they hatched, he kept the creatures in fishbowls and then in bigger and bigger bodies of water."

"That's why we were finding more and more of this," Cleo said, holding up the folded cup and pointing to its crinkly steam.

Jake gave her a grim nod. "It might look like bark," he said, "but it's shed skin."

"The beast was molting," Cleo said with a shudder, "shedding its skin, and growing."

"A successful fish business requires loyal workers," Moxie said, "and a steady supply of food, so Hangfire preyed on the schoolchildren of Stain'd-by-the-Sea. They stole honeydew melons to feed the young animals they were taking care of. Eventually the creatures would get old enough to feed on the children themselves. Hangfire nursed and nurtured his plan, waiting patiently and quietly. He knew that soon the entire town would be under his control, once he had the statue that could make the beasts do his bidding."

"Beast*s*?" asked Pocket, the *s* hissing in the air. "You mean there's more than one?"

"I don't know," I admitted. "Perhaps it has many siblings. I tried to read more about the harvesting of aquatic creatures, but the book that contained the most important secrets was destroyed."

Moxie opened her typewriter, and finally looked me in the eye. "That book was destroyed because of you," she said, "and you destroyed Hangfire, too. You murdered him, Snicket. You

269

didn't have to feed him to that creature, but you did."

The crowd frowned and murmured. "With Hangfire gone," I said, "the Inhumane Society will fall apart. There will be nobody to keep the schoolchildren drugged and imprisoned at Wade Academy, and his treacherous plot of revenge will no longer hang over Stain'd-by-the-Sea, and the town can rise again."

The woman with the dented suitcase looked around the lonely landscape. "How?" she asked.

"With a brilliant chemist," I told her, "whose formula for invisible ink can rescue the town's industry from ruin. With a skilled cook who can feed those hungry for food, and an excellent journalist who can feed those hungry for information. With a sculptor learning to fight fires from the uncles who are raising her, and two brave and resourceful siblings who can learn from the mistakes of their mother."

Sharon gasped and pointed at the air. We

all stopped and listened. It was the bell at the top of the tower at Wade Academy. Even with Hangfire gone, someone was ringing the all-clear. "And a generation of schoolchildren," I finished with a smile, "freed from the Wade Academy, who can help return this town to its law-abiding ways."

Pip gave me a cautious smile. "And I suppose my brother and I," he said, "can drive all these noble people around."

"I hope you'll do more than just that," I said. "Stain'd-by-the-Sea no longer has a librarian, not even a sub-librarian. But you two are some of the most voracious readers I know. You've never taken money from me, only book recommendations, and you know where we hid the books when the library was wrecked."

"In the attic of Black Cat Coffee," Squeak said. "That cupboard's a lot larger than it looks."

"You can restore the library," I said, "keep the books safe from the Farnsworth Pulpeater moths, and keep the accounts of my time in this town safe and accessible."

"What accounts?" Pip asked.

"The ones I plan on writing," I said. "It's a fragmentary plot, so I can't send my complete report to one place. That way the history of these times can't be destroyed in one blow." I turned my gaze to the three adult librarians, and the two future librarians who would continue the work of Dashiell Qwerty. "Walleye, Pocket, Eratosthenes, Bellerophons—I will send you some materials."

"You can send it to us," Walleye said, with a cautious nod. "Paper will put up with anything that's written on it. You can send us whatever answers you have found."

"Not answers," I said. "Questions. I'll send you each some questions," and if you are reading these reports then you know they received them.

"Giacomo Casanova had a turn," Pocket said. "Marcel Duchamp had a turn. Beverly

Cleary had a turn. Librarians have done difficult things for more or less noble reasons. It's our turn now. We are witnesses to your story, Lemony Snicket."

Eratosthenes nodded. "But we weren't witnesses to Qwerty's murder. We'll tell those police officers what we really saw."

"We'll tell everyone," Walleye said, turning his bald head to look at everyone gathered around us. "There was a murder on *The Thistle of the Valley* this evening," he said, "and the murderer forced us to lie about it."

"A child burst into our compartment through the window," Pocket replied, "and told us there'd be three more dead librarians if we didn't tell the police that Theodora was the murderer."

"That Markson woman was framed," Eratosthenes said. "She should be released from her cell."

"She will be," came the voice of Harvey Mitchum, as he walked forward with his wife, "now that we have the real criminal in custody."

"We caught Qwerty's murderer just as she was trying to slip away," Mimi said, and the Mitchums parted like heavy, sweaty curtains to reveal Ellington Feint. Her green eyes were stormy, and her hands seemed to glint in the dim light as she held her bag. Stew lurked behind her like a shadow, although shadows rarely smirk at the people around them.

"This is wrong," Walleye said, pointing at Ellington, and it was only then that I saw Ellington was in handcuffs. "She's not the murderer."

"It's that boy behind her," Pocket said.

"Yes," Eratosthenes said, and pointed one of his long and bony fingers at Stew Mitchum. "He's the one."

The Mitchums could not look at each other, or at their son. "You'll leave our boy alone," Harvey said quietly.

"He's a good boy," Mimi said. "He's never given us an ounce of trouble."

"He's as adorable as he is innocent," Harvey Mitchum agreed.

"And innocent as he is adorable," his wife agreed.

"We're not going to arrest our own son," Harvey said.

"It's not natural," his wife agreed. "It's this Ellington girl who committed murder."

"She's always been a suspicious character."

"She's a bad egg."

"A dreadful influence on the community," Harvey said.

"You're wrong," I said to Mimi Mitchum.

"Don't tell her she's wrong," Harvey said to me. "I'm the one who tells my wife when she's wrong."

"You're wrong about that," said Mimi to her husband.

"How can you call me wrong?"

"Because you are wrong, Harvey."

"You're wrong about that, Mimi."

"I'm wrong about your being wrong, but you're not wrong about calling me wrong? Only a sofa cushion would think that made sense."

"Only a lampshade would say that," Harvey said. "You're saying the wrong things and you're saying them wrong."

"*Incorrectly*," Mimi corrected, and I turned from them and looked at Ellington. Tendrils of seaweed from the Clusterous Forest waggled at me behind her. So much danger, I thought, staring into that vast and lawless place. So much danger, and the Mitchums of the world just bicker. "You're letting a murderer go free," I said, and now Ellington raised her eyes to look at me.

"You're a murderer yourself," she said, her mouth curled with fury. "You've been tricking me since the night we met, in order to push me in the right direction. You knew all along, didn't you? You knew Hangfire was my father."

I reached out to her, and she moved violently

away from me. I had to grab the chain that bound her hands, in order to look into her eyes. Her curled eyebrows had always reminded me of question marks, but now they just looked furious. You'll never see Ellington Feint smile again, I thought to myself, but it was a moment before I could bring myself to reply. "I hoped it wasn't true," I said finally.

"You could have told me what you knew," she said.

I looked at the statue in my other hand. "You could have told me what you had," I said.

"You killed him," she said. Her voice was a wild whisper.

"He was a villain," I said.

"He was my father," Ellington said. "You promised to help me, and you murdered him instead."

"I think I kept my promise," I said, but the Mitchums stepped into the middle of our argument.

"Unhand her, lad," Harvey Mitchum said firmly. "This girl is under arrest for the murder of Dashiell Qwerty."

"You can't arrest her," I said. "She didn't kill him."

"We say she did," Mimi Mitchum said, and her son smirked and nodded.

"We're letting your chaperone out of jail, Snicket," Harvey said, and tried to pry my hand loose from the little chain, "but this girl is coming with us."

"We'll stop you," I said, hanging on as hard as I could.

"*We?*" Stew repeated scornfully. "You look all alone to me, Snicket."

I looked around, but no one around looked back. Jake and Cleo were staring off at the Clusterous Forest. Ornette was looking back in the direction of town. The Haines family couldn't take their eyes off one another, now that they were together, and Pip and Squeak were staring in confusion at each other, now that they had heard what had happened. Moxie was the only one who met my eyes, and then after a moment she looked back at the page she was typing.

"Snicket," she said gently, "Ellington Feint has been helping Hangfire from the moment she arrived in town. She deserves to be in a prison cell."

"But not for murder," I said. "You know the truth, Moxie."

"I'm typing up the truth," she told me.

"But it's more than a matter of journalism," I said. "It's a matter of law."

She shook her head. "I don't think so," she said. "I think it's a matter of handcuffs." And Moxie Mallahan was right. Mimi kept tugging my hand away, and then Harvey stepped in to help, and when Stew put his grimy hand in and began tugging at the handcuffs, my own hands fell away and Ellington Feint was under their control.

My eyes fell on Gifford and Ghede. Gifford was looking at his watch, and Ghede was looking at Gifford's watch too. "Can't you help?" I asked, but they were already shaking their heads.

"Not our job, Snicket," Gifford said.

"What is your job," I asked, "besides poisoning my tea?"

"We told you our jobs," Ghede said, "and you mucked up our plan but good."

"What do you mean?"

" 'But good' is a phrase you can put at the end of a sentence to give it particular emphasis," Gifford said. "Someday we'll explain it to you but good."

"Explain it now," I said. "Explain everything now."

Ghede reached out and straightened my collar, as if she couldn't help pretending to be my mother, even after all this time. "You derailed more than a train," she said. "You derailed a grand scheme, in which everyone had a job to do. The engineer's job, for instance, was to make an unscheduled stop. The job of the police was to guard the prisoners. The conductors' job was to keep track of all the passengers. Hector is surveying an icy mountain lake, and Widdershins is in a submarine deep underwater. Josephine is delivering a message to Monty, and Beatrice is accompanying Olaf to the edge of a strange forest. All the volunteers are doing their jobs—all of us except you. You threw a wrench in the works, Snicket. Instead of drinking your tea like a good boy, you left your sister to do a two-person caper all alone, and now you've mucked up our job of making sure no one interfered with the volunteers on board."

"Well, you failed," I said. "All the volunteers have been interfered with. Dashiell Qwerty is dead and Theodora was arrested."

"You're wrong, Snicket," Gifford said, but I was already stalking off to see. I followed close behind the Mitchums as they trooped back to

The Thistle of the Valley, jangling their keys and dragging their prisoner onto the train and down the corridor of the prison car. Ellington looked at nothing but the floor. It doesn't matter if you never see someone again, I told myself. There are millions of people in the world, and most of them never see each other in the first place. You hoped to know Ellington Feint forever, but there's no such thing as forever, really. Everything is much shorter than that. When we reached the cell door, the Officers Mitchum both tried to use their keys at the same time and argued over it, so Stew had time to give me a nasty smile before his parents opened the heavy, clumsy lock. The cell door creaked open, and there stood S. Theodora Markson, my chaperone, her hands still cuffed and her hair still ridiculous. It seemed like a long time since I'd seen her.

"Lemony Snicket," she said to me. "What are you doing?"

"S. Theodora Markson," I said. "What does the S stand for?"

She frowned at me and at the Mitchums. "Surely there's an explanation for this," she said.

"You're free to go," Harvey Mitchum told her, "and that's all we have to say to you."

"We also say, don't come back to Stain'd-by-the-Sea," Mimi said.

"And," her husband said, "you should be ashamed of yourself."

"And come on out," Mimi said, but when Theodora came on out I was so startled I almost jumped. I made myself stop myself.

Breathe, I thought. Breathe and keep still, Snicket.

There are times when you're so wrong that you can't even be right about how wrong you really are. All my wrong questions came crashing together like a derailed train. This was the right cell, where Theodora had been, and she hadn't been here alone. I had been told this. I had been told there were more volunteers on the train, but it hadn't meant anything to me until this moment, holding the statue and letting Ellington go. The other prisoner stood there too. She kept still and breathed. We'd learned at school not to talk to each other, not to recognize each other, if circumstances demanded it.

Kit Snicket and I stood and thought about each other.

The Officers Mitchum gave Ellington a little push, and she stumbled her way into the cell. She looked back at me, but they slammed the door before she could say anything but my name. Behind her I saw my sister extending her hand, as she did whenever she met someone new. The locks clanked into place. Ellington had her bag with her. My sister was good with a skeleton key. Soon they would know each other. I could do nothing more.

"Now get out of the prison car," Harvey Mitchum said, "and get out of town."

"And stay away from our child," Mimi said.

"Mimi," Harvey said with a sigh, "if he stays out of town he'll automatically stay away from Stew."

"Everyone will stay away from your son," I told them. "Bullies don't last long all by themselves. Without Hangfire, the Inhumane Society is scattering to the winds. Where does that leave Stew Mitchum?"

The boy went a little pale and stepped aside as I walked with Theodora down the corridor of the train. All three Mitchums glared at me one last time. When my chaperone and I stepped off *The Thistle of the Valley* and pushed through the seaweed at the edge of the Clusterous Forest to stand with the others, I could see that the crowd had relaxed a little bit. Most of the masks were forgotten on the ground. Kellar and

Lizzie were sitting on the fender of the taxicab, smiling and talking while their mother stood quietly by. Cleo was sketching something on a scrap of paper while the three librarians looked on. Jake was smiling at something that Pip had said, and Moxie was just finishing with a page of type, and I could see Sally Murphy walking amongst some of the other passengers, offering to sign autographs. But when they saw me return, everything stopped and everyone stared. They stared and they shivered. I walked amongst them like a moving shadow, casting darkness over everyone I knew. Gifford and Ghede were the only ones who approached me, but they didn't give me as much as a glance, and talked right over my head.

"Your apprentice's foolishness has derailed our plan," Gifford said to Theodora, gesturing to *The Thistle of the Valley*. "We need to get this whole thing back on track."

"There's work to be done," Ghede said, with a nod. "Every capable adult will need to help us."

"And me," Theodora added, with a hairy nod. "Snicket, talk to the people here and see if anyone has some rubber bands. I'll supervise while you braid them together into a towing rope."

"You'll have to do that yourself," I said. "My apprenticeship is over."

She frowned at me. "What?"

"I said my apprenticeship is over."

"I heard you the first time, Snicket," she said, and looked at Gifford and Ghede. "I'm afraid my apprentice is at a difficult age."

"Maybe he needs a nap," Gifford said. "He's probably on his last legs, an expression which here means you're a tired boy."

"We're all on our last legs," I said. "We don't start out as eggs, or tadpoles. These are the only legs I'm ever going to have."

"You're talking nonsense," Ghede said, looking at me at last. "You'll go with us back to the city, where you should have been in the first place."

"No," I said, "and you heard me the first time."

Theodora frowned at me. "Be sensible, Snicket. Be proper."

"I'm not old enough," I said, and walked away, away from my chaperone and her associates and the whole mess that concerned them. My own associates saw me, but they didn't say anything. Nobody did. I would have liked it if they'd said something, but I do not volunteer expecting gifts or thanks in return. It was not necessary for the denizens of Stain'd-by-the-Sea to help me, just as it was not necessary for me to tell them all I knew. I knew that Moxie's mother would never send for her, just as I knew Pip and Squeak's father was gone forever. I knew that Kellar and Lizzie were going to help each other, and that Jake and Cleo were lucky to have found each other. But it was not necessary to say such things. It was not necessary to say anything at all. My heart ached to say something to them, but it wasn't my job.

I just gave them a wave, which here meant "so long." They gave me a wave back, which could have meant anything at all.

I walked for some time along the train tracks, with the dark statue of the Bombinating Beast tucked into my coat. Long ago, I had made a promise to return the statue to its rightful owner. The sky was getting lighter and I was whistling the tune Ellington had played me, first on a Hangfire phonograph and then on a music box her father had given her. She had not told me the name of the tune. It was a mystery, like what the *S* stood for in Theodora's name. I kept walking, with nothing but solitude for company. "Solitude" is a fancy name for being all by yourself. It's not a bad name, I thought.

The Clusterous Forest kept rustling and shivering on the other side of the tracks, and from time to time I looked into its thick and swirling depths, until at last I found a place that had been cleared a little. There was even a small path, winding its way into the seaweed and disappearing within its whisperings. I stood and thought. I thought about my sister, and I thought about my chaperone and my other associates and the people of Stain'd-by-the-Sea, and last of all I thought about Ellington Feint. I wondered what she'd known about her father. I wondered if villainy was like Armstrong Feint, someone once kind and gentle who lowered himself into treachery, or more like a mysterious beast, hidden in the depths and summoned to wickedness. But all these questions seemed wrong. They weren't my job. Like Hector and Widdershins, like Josephine and Monty and the rest of my associates, my job was not to ask questions about villainy, but to try and repair its damage.

I turned and kept moving. I walked away from the city, where I'd had my early training, and I walked away from Stain'd-by-the-Sea, where I no longer belonged. I walked away from the tracks and into the wild and lawless territory of the Clusterous Forest. I moved quickly. I moved quietly. The beast shivered in my coat. My apprenticeship was over, but there was still work to be done.

LEMONY SNICKET has ridden the rails, gotten off track, and lost his train of thought. His investigative research has been collected and published in books, including those in *A Series of Unfortunate Events* and *All the Wrong Questions*.

If **SETH** has any regrets about working with Lemony Snicket, it's clear now that train has left the station. Seth is a multi-award-winning cartoonist, author, and artist, whose works include *Palookaville*, *Clyde Fans*, and *The Great Northern Brotherhood of Canadian Cartoonists*. He lives in Guelph, Canada.